EROS ISLAND

EROS ISLAND

TONY HANANIA

BLOOMSBURY

First published 2000

Copyright © 2000 by Tony Hanania

The moral right of the author
has been asserted

Bloomsbury Publishing Plc, 38 Soho Square,
London W1V 5DF

A CIP catalogue record for this
book is available from the British Library

ISBN 07475 4737 8

10 9 8 7 6 5 4 3 2 1

Typeset by Palimpsest Book Production Limited,
Polmont, Stirlingshire
Printed by Clays Ltd, St Ives plc

To my father, Farid Hanania, a generous teacher

Dios y Madre
Arena, Sangre
Olvidan siempre
Por islas de amor

Canciones de Exilo

CONTENTS

SYLVIE

1997
SEPTEMBER

You told me in this life all our desires are fulfilled on condition they do not bring the happiness we expected of them.

And still sometimes in those late summers when I returned from the island you would drive in from the house Don Luis had bought by the river at Richmond, and we would meet in the afternoons at a cinema in Kensington or Notting Hill Gate, and always you would bring your baby boy swaddled in a hooded anorak despite the heat, and afterwards we would sit out what time we had left in one of those new coffee bars crowded with tourists and fashionable shoppers on the vivid promenades of those same blocks which a dozen years before had been that wild and forgotten hinterland of rooming-houses and derelict squares where I had stalked your ghosts as a goat bites at the moon.

And always you would appear not to have made an effort, against a waning tan your hasty gash of lipstick, moccasins with unmodishly faded jeans never quite loose enough to conceal your gentle hefts, the sun-latticed geography of your sharp face like the prospect of territory lost in war, no closer than the view through my father's binoculars in the last years before he retired to the island, borderland wadis and forbidden villages, under the indifferent bluffs the fissures of wild poppies and streets of grass.

And in your eyes the silent pleading of a prisoner without reprieve and of course we could have driven back to the flat and for a couple of hours clung together and wept, but afterwards I would not have held you, over the sour heat of the street the fruit ripening under striped awnings, through the estate the jangle of an ice-cream van, my back to the bed at the window so I would not have to watch the furtive calculations of your leaving.

But on that afternoon you were late for the performance, across the stub-pocked carpet of the empty foyer a silver glare from the entrance-hall, at the counter a girl reading alone, a spread of softening brownies and carrot cakes, over the high window posters of forthcoming releases, a Kieslowski Memorial double-bill, a spoof Sixties spy film, the rigid suaveness of the star with pistol and gloves crossed over his chest like the effigy of a Pharaoh bearing his golden sceptres, his glamorous assistant in diminutive scale, as if a vassal queen.

Rose had thinned down since the years I had known her, the withered party balloon of her leather cat-suit black and viscous as the prunes in their juice my father would be stewing over a low fire as under the cover of the trellis-hoops I returned from the nightclubs down the coast, over the terrace the drained pool and the villas on the fairways lit as if from within in the candy-rose glow of the island dawn.

As we had missed the film we drove to see what remained of the spectacle in the park, and when we passed the last of the shops you told me the death of the princess had emptied every florist and market-garden on the continent, all the mourning-blooms imported from Israel; on the paths nearest the road the usual thin carnival of roller-bladers and summer students playing with kites, but through the line of beeches the smell of harvests left rotting in fields, and towards the gardens we could see stooped figures gently carrying away the dead bouquets, the volunteers in khaki overalls and white masks as if at the site of an industrial accident, and beyond the wide floe of flowers the mounds of those already turning to mulch like the ashes of a great pyre.

Against the railings were stacked the newly laid bouquets, teddy-bears, paper angels, cards of valediction, photographs of the princess, and when we came to the diptyches with her final lover you did not recall the sullen young man we had always avoided at the parties in the hills, his nose wet as a puppy, his bloodless lips, his restless disregard for the necklaces of light over the plains of the city, his face here like the mountain icons of those venal youths of whom death had made saints whose worldly eyes seemed still to mock the pious widows climbing the sheer paths to lay coins and sweetbreads at their shrines.

But you do not stay to look, and without kissing me walk away among the tourists and leaping dogs to the road, the face of the little boy staring back, his dark features hidden under the fur fringes of the hood as you turn his head towards a kite riding in the gusts above the trees.

Slowly you disappear behind the line of beeches, through the shadows heavy with the scents of the flowers the echo of one small voice.

Rock-rose, lilies, blue lupins.

From the house the family walking through the olive orchards to Bethlehem, waist-deep in the high grass your Aunt Anastasia picking posies, rock-rose, blue iris, mountain lilies, rosemary, hollyhocks, anemones blood-red as the buttons on the gown of the bride; under the shade of the holm oak Jamila the maid lifting the broad fig leaves draped over the basket, on the gingham cloth laying sambusek, jibneh, white plums, the coins on her bonnet like the quiver of a tambourine in the breeze through the rifts, your Uncle Anton standing apart from the others, the trousers of his pressed vanilla suit rolled above his knees, his wide-brimmed

7

boater lowered against the high sun, and below on the ridge your Uncle Pascal, my twin, peering out through his box-camera to the sunken dome, the tomb of Rachel which the legend says was built by Jacob when his wife died in childbirth on this old road to Canaan, and beyond in the distance through the dust on the valley the massed tents of the Turkish troops wide as the white dunes of the deserts to the south.

These details smooth and polished as the amber worry-beads he turns in the shadows, a soukh-trader sifting for false coins, as always the curtains closed against the drained pool; over the beach the narrowed panorama of golf links and villa crescents and condominiums; under the breakwater, a camper-van, a smouldering bonfire.

And their tents wide as the white dunes of the deserts to the south, on the carossa along the road from Ramleh the skirts of the maids lifting like churned smeed in the stronger winds down the wadis, the strange ruin of a giant stone honeycomb with a charred hollow where the tuberculosis doctor had stacked his patients until one had been burnt alive, returning to the dusty avenues of Mamilla lined with shrivelled plane trees which cast no shade, through the garden gates glimpses of the shimmering dome above the walls of the old city, our burnished bronze orange-squeezer, the juice cooled with shavings from the ice-house in the cellars where they store the crates from the orchards of orange and clementine on the shores of the Dead Sea, above the terraces the scaffolding over the excavations, the road winding back up the valley on to seas of sand infinite as the darkening sky.

For the fifteen years since we had left the burning city my father had rarely strayed from the scuffed leather armchair under the shuttered french windows which were never opened to the unswept terrace above the drained pool, and when I sat with him in the half-light he would speak only of those years long ago in Jerusalem, and never of Beirut where all the family had fled as refugees apart from my uncle the photographer who had his own reasons for staying behind.

I remembered little of the city other than the house and the gardens which I had been forbidden to leave. With the drone of the generators and the incessant hooting in the neighbouring streets I heard nothing of the first battles over the headland, and the high breccia walls draped with rank wisteria hid the prospects of the smoke-shrouded skies to the south.

And all I could remember of the house was what I had feared. When the gardeners no longer came the tall grass concealed the coils of discarded snake skins fine as the gauze of surgical stockings, among the tall old books warped and mildewed from sea travel in the illuminated volume of Jules Verne the pictures of the undersea mummies grey as the caterpillar hives in the stone pines spilling their long thin files of brown-backs over the dust-blown lawns into the weave of a vast net lifting the house and the gardens high above the burning skies of the city.

And from behind the casement bays of the front study I saw the old people come through the gates and stand under the steps to the porch, tentative and expectant as passing beggars, the stooped woman with her hollow, sleepless eyes, and the thin man in his scarecrow-loose linen suit and stained old-style rounded cuffs, the long noble face he held up like a mask on the head of his cane always strangely familiar, and the two were never allowed beyond the verandah, and on the days they called I would be sent to my room and watch from the cover of the deep bays; my father hastily handing out those bills he had in his pocket, and closing the door.

I do not know that I was ever told of the death of my uncle in Jerusalem, but as long as I could remember the door to the room where his possessions were stored had always been kept locked. On the afternoons my father had gone out and the maid was sleeping I would slip the latch between the outer shutters and drop down over the ledge into the darkness, the cool tiles like a slap against my bare soles.

The room was almost bare, no jackets or coats in the wardrobes, a row of wire hangers, the spent larvae of the unzipped suit bags, on the shelves the charcoal card pages of the albums empty but for the plastic corners and dark rectangles like groundplans for buildings never constructed.

Beside the cupboard the antique cameras with their jack-in-the-box lenses, lilting tripods like drill-rigs, their shadows against the shuttered glare the legs of giant insects, and beyond along the wall old flaps and drops, the fading façade of a rococo palace, a willow-sheltered pond under a silver moon, a balustrade before a distant view of snow-turbaned mountains.

The last retouched, framed. Over the white sands of a deserted bay, a white villa below hills of umbrella pines.

Above the albums, a locked casket of olive wood inlaid with mother-of-pearl, the letters or photographs within clattering like the wings of the sea pigeons trapped in the chimney above the fireplace we never used.

And standing in that dim airless room with the skein of white light over the peeling plaster I would see again a vision of a golden dome above high walls, but when I told my father of this strange memory always he would assure me we had lived in no other house.

1982, 1981

I

Some songs are so much of their moment that to be true to themselves they must disappear without trace, stones cast into a deep lake, but when today in a bar or a crowded shop I hear by chance one of the lesser numbers of those years always I will breathe again the mown grass and the young green bracken along the lanes of that last summer at school when the boys were prettier than the girls and through the warm late afternoons lay out in their frilly white shirts and piratical breeches on the banks of the river pubs where the masters did not patrol and in the cover of the willow gardens.

The school itself lay beside water-meadows under chalk downs, to the west hills of wheat and barley built over with crescents of commuter homes, the long grey nave and squat tower of the cathedral divided by a tidy close and flint walls from the medieval library and classroom annexes; in the neighbouring streets the red-brick dormitory houses, their cellars converted into studies for the senior boys.

I shared with Palgrave, through the sunken barred window overgrown with nettles and cow-parsley a cribbed view of the croquet lawn, untended rose beds, marrow runs. The walls of his half bare, on the shelves above his desk, biographies of Rimbaud, Auden, Wilde. Over my patched chaise-longue, frayed Beardsley posters, photographs of maverick tennis stars hung at waggish angles, a collage of Ilie Nastase touch-strokes, and my only photograph of Sylvie which I had stolen from the cork board above the fireplace in her tower-den at the house in the hills on my last vacation to the the island; clasping her narrow shoulders, she shivers under the lava heads on the north coast where I had never been.

The study-hall above the room, a maze of work-pews carved with antique graffiti, corner cubicles built up with chipboard and bricks and mattresses into shanty dwellings, the juniors in their black gowns perched like crows on the curtain-rails calling obscenities across a wasteland of broken glass, stray shoes, foil wrappers. Beside the panelled door to the study of the housemaster, the high roll of the fallen in its pilastered cartouche, a long trestle-table grooved and ash-black as an ancient sacrificial altar, the jingoistic headlines of the unread newspapers slowly rotting under the rancid overflow from the milk bottles.

Only if we had missed the meals in the refectory would we come up to the hall to receive our tribute from the tuck-boxes of the juniors, Palgrave tearing out clippings on the Cambridge Structuralist Controversy which he hid behind his biographies with his imported editions of Barthes and Blanchot while I sought passing release in the summary wanding of a junior before the inevitable descent to the unabridged Morte D'Arthur with its tapestry of quests spliced and devious as tracks over wet dunes.

It was in the late afternoons when the juniors were at games that we would venture out through the cathedral close to take coffee at the Royal Hotel on the far side of the High Street, an old coaching inn expanded during the late eighteenth century and still retaining a certain muted gentility; Palgrave as always in his Wildean uniform, a long astrakhan coat and his lime carnation soaked overnight in a pot of green Quink ink.

The head porter was known as Jesus on account of his lank straight hair and open-toed sandals, and had been bribed by the inner circle of the previous generation of seniors to bar other boys from entering the hotel, and so after further bribes to secure our own admittance we were to find we had the place almost entirely to ourselves. We took our coffee in the conservatory, along the inner walls potted palmettos and ferns, the polished bronze of the table-tops reflecting the glare through the dull panes between the picked bones of the elaborate apex of white joists and struts, the french windows overlooking a walled garden, an unevenly trimmed lawn narrowing to gravel paths between ruined pergolas and moss-encrusted statues.

In these quiet surroundings the notorious inner circle had sequestered themselves from the remainder of the school. We explored their abandoned domain like peasants in the palace of a fallen tyrant. Though they had left two years before, their memories already turning to myth. In the shadow-streaked hall we sought out Reaper's Retch, so toxic that like the blood of Banquo it would never be cleansed; among the study-pews it was said the stain had assumed the precise form of the northern coastline of the island. We found nothing, and I could not reconcile the dapper dandy I still recalled strolling in his velvet-collared crombie and tasselled silk scarf through the close with the vile deeds by which he was remembered.

In the rear of the conservatory we searched for Foley's Frescos, his illustrations from the Satyricon rendered during a mescalin trip on a rare excursion from the sick bay where he passed his days tended by the young Nigerian nurses he had corrupted, his ingenious ailments personified in the finely drawn cartoons which festooned the walls of his oval ward overlooking the water-meadows. But the length of the lower wall had been emulsioned over, and covered by high-back settles.

From the first-floor landing we spied into the Ozzy Rustum Suite, hired for the duration of the term by the only son of a dynasty of exiled Tehrani Jewish financiers to entertain exotic whores from London for the pleasure of Anna Bloom, the louche belle of St Swithun's, the girls' boarding-school on the hill to the east of the town.

Anna Bloom was believed to have been mistress to all three of the inner circle, her gossiped depravity so firing my imagination that as a junior I had once prevailed upon my father on one of his infrequent visits to stay at the hotel in the hope of a glimpse of the legendary sybarite, but that afternoon all I had witnessed were two spinsters taking tea, and across the hallway in the low-lit bar the slumped figure of Rustum dozing in his tweed suit over a history of the still life.

After the closed dinners of the inner circle in the rear conference room rumours of strange rites and panelling smeared with blood and faeces would for months circulate the study-pews, but we had found only empty cartouches and the smooth amber of old varnish, the long table already laid with place-cards and replicate bouquets for the next private function.

Those boys without the funds to bribe their way past Jesus habituated a coffee house at the upper end of the High Street under a genteel teashop of the same name owned by the retired Major Lovell and his wife, through the bottle-glass window on frilly-fringed doilies the staggered display of homemade quiches and cakes, a separate entrance descending from the street into the barrel-vaulted cellar, a single row of stained-pine tables under the bare brick walls, the flapjacks and tepid coffee brought down the cast-iron stairway by the only daughter of the Major, Rose, a busty punkette with a snout-ring and tartrazine hair who had been expelled from St Swithun's the year before in undisclosed circumstances and would spend her breaks smoking roll-ups with the braves in the arcade outside Woolworths.

The dour surroundings brought up the livid cerises and scallop-pinks of the cravats and foulards of Gervase Webb and his retinue of fops who slouched with their copies of Gide and Fitzgerald in the furthest recesses of the cellar, though their talk was always strictly limited to questions of sartorial decorum, the measure and fall of collars and cuffs, the prosody of the buttonhole.

Sometimes when Palgrave was studying I would tag along with Webb through the alleys of half-timbered souvenir shops to his fittings at Gieves & Hawkes on the north side of the cathedral, the oriel window of the upstairs room looking down over the Green, tattooed squaddies swilling beer, tourists wandering among the headstones: infinite reflections in the glass-fronted cabinets and tall chevals; a thin tailor chalking in the cuts and tucks; dummies, off-cuts; a young girl with her imp face and spiked strawberry-blonde bob holding scissors and tape-measures; like Fate with her eternal attributes.

And afterwards as we walked back across the close Webb would claim this girl was the daughter of a legendary pop star whom he did not name, serving her apprenticeship in lining and cutting before going up to design school in London, but I dismissed this notion, as I did the rumours that the Major's daughter had been expelled for working the pubs on the estate to feed a drug habit for I knew Webb took a secret and deliberate pleasure in the dissemination of false gossip whose warping circulation he would monitor and relish only to blame its invention on his original confidant.

Palgrave was an idol to Webb and the other fops, but abjured their company. His was a private archaeology of the dandy. Arlen, Acton; Beardsley, Whistler, Wilde; Huysmans, Montesquieu-Fezensac, Nerval; Beau

Brummell; his archive of monographs, drawings, postcards in the locked drawer he would open only when I was practising over on the grass courts.

Palgrave sought out the living filaments to his lost world. In the vacation he made the pilgrimage to La Pietra, and later he would return to the grave of Acton at the Cimitero Inglese on the industrial outskirts of the Via Servese; on that quiet stretch of wall beneath the arches, laying eleven white lilies below the simple grey plaque.

Some weekends the Warden of All Souls would sit out on the bank above the boys playing croquet, and all afternoon from the study window Palgrave would closely study the ailing aesthete, his eyes wide and unblinking as the magnifying lenses of the juniors who crouched on the lower lawns waiting for fire.

Palgrave insisted I accompany him to poetry readings. In the bright oak-panelled room on College Street we listened to Andrew Motion read a long poem about the flatlands; the ivory bangle on his hairless wrist like the hoops thrown for furry pierrots at the island ferias where I had searched in vain for Sylvie.

Palgrave did not deign to attend regular lessons, only those of the young English literature master, Lachlan Mackinnon; in his class on Shakespeare I had ventured a derivative view on the 'Great Chain of Being', he had retorted 'Clank, clank', and I had never dared speak up again. But Palgrave had told me that this master was a secret poet, and had remained in confidential contact with other 'Sherpas of Parnassus'.

At weekends we would take the train to Waterloo Station, and make our pilgrimage from the Chelsea Arts Club via Jules Cocktail Bar on Jermyn Street to the Café Royal, but all we found were noisome bankers and Sloane Rangers out on the razzle, not a poet in sight. In previous years Palgrave had muled wraps for Rustum from a barbiturate-amputee at the Dilly to fund his collection of prints and monographs, and sometimes if we had a score between us we would search out one of the old-timers who still hung about the alleys under the gambling dens off Gerrard Street, and after we had chased in the Gents' on the corner wander up to Soho, against the sepia sky the winged god with his outstretched bow diving over the square like a great bird of prey, at the Colony Rooms, Bacon and Proctor and the other old queens always good for a drink; we would return on the last train, our heads spinning in the carriage-lights as the dim film of terraces and commuter towns spilled into the still dark cornfields of Hampshire.

On those nights we avoided the patrols of masters across the Green and the grids of streets between the dormitory houses and the town, following the back way from the station to the one late-night bistro above the High Street, the walls hung with antique enamel advertisements and posters of the Moulin Rouge; the tables around the bar lit by candles in wax-streaked champagne bottles, in the rear booths the girls from St Swithun's, their hair teased into spikes and forelocks, waiting to be bought drinks or taken down to the yard for a joint or a snog.

Sometimes I would go home with the daughter of a local estate agent whose name I have forgotten, the St Swithunites in their modish cream dungarees and vivid braces, but always she wore Capri pants and sequin halter-tops like a chorus girl from Grease, her flint-fronted house overlooking the low glimmer of the new commuter closes to the west of the town.

In the kitchen we were always silent so as not to wake her parents, and after the privations of the refectory I would gorge on Swiss-rolls and cooking-chocolate, and later during our drunken rut on the damp cushions in the garden shed, my face buried in her thick bob with its crust of dried mousse, and in your night sands.

II

On old maps place-names mark cities built on trade, and the ways between, fords, springs, mountain passes, a geography of leisure existing only in the imagination, lands of Cockaigne, houses of barley-sugar, streets paved with pastry, shops selling goods for nothing; the extinction of need, and compassion: such mirages of plenitude the laboratories of our future where men must wrestle with the dead hands of time.

To such a resort my father had chosen to retire.

The scree of the high sierra and the hills of cork and umbrella pine spun with the whitewash ridges of pueblo developments, on the plain the urbanisations behind their pseudo-Maghreb castellations like toy forts on the landscaped carpet of golf links, grids of rose-red tennis courts clustering over the carretera to the honeycomb marinas built up on moles reclaimed from the sea between crescent beaches of imported white sand.

The villa had been bought originally for my mother as a refuge from the humid summers, and overlooked a small bay on that southernmost coast which hung like an untucked shirt beneath the limestone belly of the island, but over the years the view along the shoreline had been lost to the rising condominiums of Bellamar, and the scrubland where the girls from the village had picked wild figs and hollyhocks to the uniform deep green of the fairways spanning out from the clubhouse; over the silted reedlands of the estuary the wash-trails of the sewage sluices from the new hotels.

Along the white walls were many shelves, niches, sconces, and all were bare, as if after an iconoclasm. In the tall gloom of the unlit hall the olive-wood casket like the sarcophagus of a still-born prince. The french windows on to the unswept terrace all locked, the shutters down, under the rusted railings the drained pool; unplanted terracotta urns and troughs choked with pine needles, gull droppings, faded litter.

All that summer my father would not leave his rooms, the household supplies brought by the maid from the SuperSol in San Roque. He would sleep behind three locked doors, and always took his revolver into the bathroom, and when I came to sit under the arc of his Anglepoise he spoke only of those years long ago in Jerusalem, and what he read remained a mystery for throughout the house I never found a single book other than those of my mother which he had left on the shelves in my room in the west wing over the beach.

I would spend my afternoons at a small tennis club in the hills, making up fours with the expatriate regulars, the quiet bar lined with pictures of the old greats, Lacoste, Perry, Laver, the tinted sliding doors opening into straw-shaded pathways above the staggered levels of the courts.

I had been learning Spanish at school but could make little of the young barman's hissing Andaluz, we struck up one of those light summer rapports between strangers; when the regulars had left we would rally in the failing light, and sit up under the umbrella pines smoking porritos, laughing at jokes we did not understand, looking down over the dim contours of the courts to the distant lights of the coastal resorts.

As the season drew to a close the regulars only came

towards evening when the hills had cooled, and sometimes we would take cold beers out to the court in the dead siesta hours, and have a dazed knock-up, the clay baking through the soles of our sneakers, the sun still high and blinding above the pine ridges.

One afternoon we had taken shelter in the shade of the cork tree beneath the court, and when I looked up through the heat-haze to the gallery under the clubhouse I saw we were being watched by some youths in Wayfarers and black leather jackets, squatting on the stacked-up sun-loungers, the boys swigging from spirit bottles with upside-down labels lifted from the bar, a slight young girl in jeans and a cardigan with her back to the group peering down at the court as if at something far away and indistinct.

As she turns the wisps of dark hair falling across her face, her cheeks pale as an invalid, her lost eyes narrowed against the glare off the court as if still seeking a first sign of land.

If I had passed the gang on the street in England I would have noticed nothing, but in the brightness of the empty club their sudden presence seemed both uncanny and staged, as if we had been visited by wandering players; their dark silhouettes against the burning cobalt of the sky like figures in a clerestory window, their parting deliberate and ponderous as divers leaving a wreck deep under the sea, the boy at the front with long gangling limbs and silver streaks in his hair gobbing down on to the warm clay under the umpire chair, the others shuffling with bowed heads towards the car-park, upsetting the stacked loungers, the empty bottles rolling over the sun-deck and down into the pathways between the courts.

The barman waited until they had gone, and then went to tidy up before the regulars arrived. He did not seem in the least surprised by what had happened.

I had been using a Mobylette to reach the club, but after my father had shot her dog the maid would not return to the house, and I had inherited her run-down van, the hot plastic seats always smelling of cheap scent, tangerines, soap flakes, the San Cristóbal swinging hypnotically from the rear-view mirror, its plastic beads clacking like an abacus on the rough roads.

Every afternoon I would drive the long way up through the pine hills, and wait until evening for the girl to appear again; the place always empty, the company of the barman beginning to drag.

I had become accustomed to his hissing Andaluz, and was spared no nuance of his analysis of the swing-serve of McEnroe and the relative merits of Moroccan and Lebanese, my only consolation to devise ways of leading the conversation back once more to the gang with spiked hair, and the girl.

No ha pasado nada, son así la gente, the barman always dismissing the episode in vacuous platitudes which though betraying some prior knowledge of the group implied their appearance was as a caprice of nature, of no rational origin, and better ignored.

On those days of restless boredom the resemblance of the barman to a pretty cox who had been sent down from our house the previous term would remind me that there were other ways we might have spent the empty afternoons, but any embarrassments would have prevented me returning to the only place where I might reckon on seeing her once more.

As my holiday drew to a close I began to lower my expectations of meeting the gang again. But though I had become reconciled to the likelihood that they had long returned to wherever they had come from, my day-long drives along the carretera and into the parched hills were still compassed by vague hopes.

23

Down among the narrow streets of San Roque, peering through the windows of the cafés and tapaterias patronised by the club regulars and the expatriates who had sought out villas at this quieter end of the coast.

I would go to the small marina, listen to crewing tales in the zinc bars; to the deserted polo field above the reed estuary; to the pueblo bars in the foothills beneath the fincas which had already begun to close after the season.

In the evenings I returned to the silent house; in the corner under the Anglepoise my father as always with his whisky and worry-beads, beneath the terrace the wash slicking the sand; out on the dark beach a low fire by the camper-van under the breakwater.

If he did not want to talk I would go to my room, and make as if to revise, all the old books of my mother along the shelves warped by the sea air, and like a pat card trick always opening at the same passages.

Und leise tönen im Rohr die dunkeln flöten des Herbstes . . .

Trakl; school editions of Heine, Schiller, Goethe; Schumann's Lieder; the Psalms rebound with gauze, sticking-plaster; against the spines, grains of sand; never hairs, notes, pressed petals.

In a locked reliquary frame above the shelf, the single framed photograph. It had been taken only weeks before the accident, two years and four months after my birth, and still every day I had to pretend for him, and recall the taste of her sun-blenched hair, and the wincing of her eyes.

I would wake early, closing the curtains tighter against the coming brightness, hoping to sleep an hour more. Sometimes I looked out over the beach, a crepuscular light between the upper dunes, in the distance a tall figure walking a motorbike unsteadily above the tideline; he would slip, and lie behind a rift before picking up the handlebars and continuing his uncertain progress, and there were times

I would wait and he would not rise, and I would wonder if he had been there at all.

In the mornings my father kept to his study, and I would not see him before I set out on my excursions along the coast. But one morning some days before I was due to return I had overslept and woke to a disturbance under the terrace, the new maid shrieking by the poolhouse, my father with his revolver, the ancient gardener shaking his rake after a naked figure running out on to the beach.

The man had doubled back and hidden behind the breakwater, pulling on his damp clothes, panting like an old dog; over the wall the silver streaks in his dripping hair; it was clear from the empty glow in his eyes that he had not recognised me from the club.

He explained he had been trying to use the shower in the poolhouse, and I apologised for my father, and walked with him across the damp dunes to the camper-van at the head of the beach.

As he jumped on the kick-start the wheels of the Montessa slowly sinking into the dune. All that day a fine rain falling over the pine hills.

I offered to drive the boy into San Roque, and once we were out on the carretera he asked me to drop him at the run-down urbanisation beyond the first marina.

At the end of the dirt-track, a large washed-out sign, El Paraíso. He said he would walk, but I assured him I was in no hurry; all morning we waited on overgrown drives to peeling bungalows for someone who did not arrive.

Outside the condensed windows, the muted churn of the waves, chuchos barking in the lanes between the empty seafront villas, no one passing. The boy told me he was called Shaman, he had run away from home. He handed me a folded photograph of an eagle circling over cork groves; he said that one day he would be a famous artist.

Eventually we gave up at the urbanisation, and continued

on the carretera into San Roque. It was the siesta hour, the streets deserted, along the lower pavements dogs and old men dozing under sun-faded awnings. I sat in the car while he went up into tenements in the back streets, each time saying he would be a couple of minutes and not coming back for almost an hour, always seeming surprised when I was still there waiting.

Many of the streets I had passed before, but I had not known there was an old maze of alleys and plazitas hidden like a second heart behind the palm-lined boulevards and squares where the town paraded at dusk.

Towards evening we parked at the edge of a wasteground looking down on a crowded bar under a cracked stucco façade that could only be approached by foot or on a scooter, and when he returned his eyes were wide, his gangling body suddenly charged with new purpose.

'You want to check a party?' His voice had lost its former slur, but still it was as if he was always talking to himself.

'Up in the hills, at Anna-and-Sylvie.' He seemed to assume I would already know where this was, and when I faltered he directed me between the unfinished but occupied tenements and one-room marisquerías along the seafront, and out on to the carretera.

We followed the road to the club through the umbrella pines, and climbed into the hills, higher up we could see far over the plain of San Roque, and beyond the salt-flats the east face of the rock sheer from the sea like the cornice of some vast sunken monument rising illegibly into the even light of a more temperate world.

When the view was lost he plucked a tape from his shrivelled leather jacket, pushing it into the deck, rewinding to the beginning of the same song which I had heard playing all that previous summer term in the bistro above the High Street.

another-girl-anotherplanet-ano-ther-plaan-nn-et . . .

He balled along, bearing up out of the sun-roof, the San Cristóbal serving for percussion against the windscreen, beyond the last pueblo he waved down over high breccia walls to an unlit finca, the old queen who lived there was good for liquor, sometimes wedge; through the first months of the summer he had dossed in his poolhouse.

After he had missed the way a couple of times we came down above an old villa, a white tower and roman-tile roofs in the lee of olive terraces and tall date palms, on the high shoulders of the earth drive dropped trail-bikes, rag-top jeeps; over the crabgrass lawns a rough arc of torches, spitting in the rain.

My thigh snagging on a mudguard, my torn jeans dribbling oil and blood, already the sun setting over the gap-toothed sierra.

It was not exactly what I would have called a party, though my experience of such matters was rather narrower than I might have admitted. Sluggish heavy metal drifting out over the gardens, nobody dancing, the only group I could see huddled under the palm gazebo beside the covered pool.

On the path he was talking to another tall boy with spiked hair and long razored cedilla sideburns, but he made no attempt to introduce me. Facetious reproaches were being exchanged, I had a sense this was the person for whom we had waited in vain all morning among the bungalows.

In the house, no lights; the dim forms of intricate murals over high mansard landings. A door opening, a Filipina in a white apron crossing a long patio lined with urns and geranium-beds, her slight figure disappearing into the shadows of the colonnade.

There were winding stairs, interwoven swags and festoons painted along the walls, the music growing fainter; I was inside the white tower we had seen from the upper turning.

The stairs opening on to a rotunda, over the cream walls

posters from ski resorts, schoolbooks and fashion magazines stacked neatly below, on the azure-tiled floor the sleigh bed with its scrolled heads like a gondola drifting at anchor.

In the middle of the room, a figure sitting in the shadows. She was bent over herself, drawing tangled patterns on her jeans.

Even in the low light I could tell who it was, stagily I cleared my throat; when she peered up through her fringe I announced in a voice too loud for the room that I had come looking for plasters, my trouser-leg raised by way of explanation, but she had already gone back to her drawing.

For a moment I thought of squatting down beside her and pretending to take an interest in the work; I edged forward, her voice low and level as the speaking-clock.

'You've come to the wrong room.'

My eyes adjusting to the light as I backed towards the stairwell, under the twirling lines a dark stain spreading down from the nib towards her knee.

For a while I wandered between the urns under the colonnade, steeling myself to return with some winning witticism, but I had little experience of courting girls, and in that house of dislocations I could hardly trust myself not to come over as the worst sort of buffoon.

Down at the car, a boy with spiked hair squatting on the bonnet, the figure reeling off towards the pool, but turning as I struggle to keep my balance on the sprinkler-soaked path.

'Hi, I'm Anna. You must have come with Shaman.' It was a girl's voice, lisping, hoarse.

I waved down to her, as if in recognition.

'Collegio Roque?'

She swatted with a gloved hand at the darkening air.

'St Swithun's. Sent down.'

I went after her alongside the covered pool, over the

palm-gazebo a wilderness of wisteria and tall grasses bordered by a steep ravine falling to a dried stream, but when I reached the edge and looked across the bare gulleys there was nobody below. I called her name, the music faint behind, ahead the restless silence of the black ridge.

Slowly I walked back, through the crouching figures, under the shelter; on the drive down the warm scents of the island night.

On the last day of the summer vacation I followed the road beyond the club, and found my way again to the valley above the white villages. Although it had been night I had noted where the track crossed the mountain road between twisted moor oaks and trailed down through the olive terraces.

But when I reached the end of the track, the rusted iron-gates had been drawn between the crumbled breccia walls, the drive beyond empty, the shutters above closed up; an old gardener under the lantana bushes, their orange blooms pale in the glare of the day and the high afternoon peace of cicadas and hissing sprinklers which had sung to me all that lonely summer.

The first day of the following vacation I returned to the valley. Through the tall plane trees and date palms, the roman-tiles catching the sun over the sierra, on the tower the shutters still closed.

Later I would learn that the house had originally belonged to Lola Montez, the popular madrileña actress of the Thirties whose lacquered hair and lustrous eyes still graced floribund tins of turrón and sugared orange-peel in the old patisserias around the Plaza Mayor. But when Berny Bloom had bought the property from a local fruit exporter in the early Sixties, the villa had been almost abandoned, the gardens a wilderness, roosters at large in the lower halls and patios, the tower open to the elements; the photographs of this past dereliction hung in the poolhouse.

When the girls were still young the Blooms had spent their winters between Gstaad and the villa, but by the early Seventies they would only go down for a couple of weeks before Easter.

After Maude Bloom had died, the house had been closed for some years, and had only been used again after Bloom's second wife, Monica, had chosen to practise her decorating fancies on the unadorned walls; over the central hall incomplete prospects of mist-shrouded follies and belvederes; the stairwells clustered with skewed swags, medallions, festoons; through the lower corridors classical ambulatories in vertiginous perspectives.

To those unused to the house the initial effect was one of immediate disorientation. The more obtrusive caprices had been covered with Berber tapestries and expansive hunting scenes, but Bloom's adoration for his young wife and respect for her temper were such that he would never permit even the most confused sections to be painted over.

When Monica had become oppressed by her own creations, and preferred to spend her numerous vacations elsewhere, the girls had been given the run of the house during the summers; Anna's guests wandering stoned through the passages and halls adding their own scholia and cartoons to the classical vistas, after each party the gardener whitewashing the more offensive defacements so that gradually the decorations had assumed the appearance of ancient murals undergoing restoration.

Shaman with the silver-streaked hair had originally come down during a year out from St Martin's as Monica's assistant, but he had stayed on to help with the reconstruction of the dependencias, and had been taken up by Anna and her gang when they arrived for the summer.

That was the summer before I had strayed into their

lives, and at night Shaman would creep in tripping from the poolhouse, his eagles concealed in the eaves of belvederes, sweeping low over scumble marshes, perching on ormolu tassels, and months would pass before they were discovered, and most visitors would assume they had been there from the beginning.

Shaman had told me all this when I found him at the bar on the little square in the old town. The camper-van on the beach had been washed away in a storm, and he was sleeping on empty boats in the marina; at first I did not ask him directly about Sylvie, and preferred to let him take the conversation his own way, and pick up what I could.

But it had seemed that first day he had only wanted to talk about Monica, and already I sensed this was a woman about whom everyone spoke, and to whom no one confided. Shaman had known Monica long before she had married; they had both grown up in the same market town in West Yorkshire; 'all grey limestone and small as shit'.

Monica would later claim that her father had worked for the National Trust, but he had been a successful local funeral director, and at the age of thirteen she had been sent away to boarding-school, and she had not come home much after that; she had left school early, and worked behind the cosmetics counter in Selfridges before marrying a tax-consultant from Weybridge whom she had left for Bloom.

When Shaman had come down to help with the murals she had made him graft, fitting wall-to-wall mirrors in her dressing-room, a marble bidet in her chartreuse bathroom; his first painting job, a white line over the crabgrass which he could not cross to overlook her sunbathing down at the pool.

The following afternoon I drove the now familiar road through the pine hills to the tennis club. The barman from the summer was gone, but the regulars were there, and as

31

the youngest player I was always in demand to make up fours.

On the palm-covered terrace outside the clubhouse, a couple I had not seen before, not playing, watching. He was older than I had expected, his thin face honed on the whetstone of difficult choices, and she was much younger, spitefully pretty, her high Asiatic cheeks starved into a pure definition of themselves, her clinging tracksuit diamond white, and its glare such that lingering eyes were obliged to squint.

In his absence the regulars had preferred not to talk about Bloom, despite my probings, perhaps because his high-rolling away from the island brought home how much out to grass they all were, but now he was back they were each foisting drinks upon him, circling busily around his table, only the older wives in their white headbands and pleated skirts still holding back from Monica's dainty gravity.

During that last term when I had thought of the house in the valley I had always imagined having trouble finding the place again, and then it would be all shut up, the iron-gates still closed; up there, not a chimera, but lost to me nonetheless.

But like many couples who are not entirely comfortable alone with each other the Blooms favoured an open house during the few weeks they came to the island, and when the bar closed it was only natural for me to tag along with the regulars from the club.

Over the drive, fairy lights on the lantana bushes, and in festive squirls over the trunks of the date palms; Chinese lanterns fluttering from posts along the path up to the house.

Inside the long halls were lit with candles burning behind scallop shells, the classical prospects obscured by elaborate flourishes of tinsel and riggings of Christmas cards, and despite the warmth everyone would gather around the kindling fire where Bloom presided with his Perfecto; in her tartan two-piece, Monica bringing round the mulled wine with cloves.

Bloom was of that school of self-made men who had made a song of their own beginnings, and as his wife looked out at her still reflection in the tall french windows on those windless nights he held us with tales of his early cunning, his weaving rise from Chapel Street through the moving rocks of the spielers and the Maltese racketeers and the Hatton Garden syndicates high into the thin air of pure speculation, and it would seem the way he sung that he knew he would never find that glory again, and leaving it all behind for the clement new world he had fought his way up into had been a loss for which his wealth would never entirely console him.

And then there were the evenings when Bloom seemed weary of his own romance, and he would puff silently beside the fire, occasionally angling for some narrow information across the grain of the conversation, always matters so scrupulously dry that he appeared deliberately to practise an inverted exoticism, and though he rarely received satisfactory answers his face seemed too set in its siccity ever to communicate disappointment, or rather under the tanned rigour of the features there was always already the sour symmetry of disappointment.

It was on one of these first evenings around the fire at the villa that Bloom turned to me touching his ash into the hearth, and asked lightly as if he were requesting me to pass an object close at hand for my thoughts on the propects of the real-estate market in Beirut, and when I sniggered, obligingly I thought, he looked away through the colonnades, and when he spoke it was as if he were giving out a gardening tip, softly, without reproach, 'They didn't teach you what old Rothschild used to say, never buy until the blood is running in the streets,' and when he smiled it always came as an afterthought, his face creasing uneasily, like a dry scroll.

But the regulars also liked to ask me about the war. They followed the conflict like a marathon chess match, and after all they had time enough, and they phrased their questions to reflect their expertise. But up there in the hidden valley as the night came in over the hills, the candlelight on the tinsel over the classical vistas, the guests in their tennis whites bobbing about like cartoon spooks, the bounded waters of the Mediterranean seemed years that could never be repealed, the underground hospitals with intermittent power, the maimings, the mutilations, the shelling as remote in that secret hollow as cruel fables in an old film.

Willingly I shared this illusion. I did not blame those who made a map room of the coffee table; pretzel-sticks, Israeli divisions; the majolica ashtray, the Bekaa Valley.

But the reason I sought a dubious authority from these sessions remained hidden in the shadows at the head of the wide marble stairs. Three days before Christmas she had first appeared there, crouching with knees drawn up to her chest like a giant cicada; across the dark hall, sucking her hair, in the half-light her face tallowy from a ski-tan, as if it might suddenly melt.

If she was listening such talk could hardly interest her. If anyone noticed her there, they did not call her down. Her eyes drawn with a fatigue whose origins I constantly pondered, as the nights passed no other expression crossing her face, and I knew I would go to long and foolish pains to witness that face relent into pleasure.

Every evening I came on early from the club in a state of some agitation for fear she would not appear that night, and though I never caught the moment of her appearance, halfway through the proceedings I would peer up and there

34

she would be on her favoured step, still as a lizard in the shadows.

And when it was rumoured there was to be a party at the house on the night of the Tres Reyes I tried to lure my father out; he had abandoned his walks on the beach, his mornings spent in the locked study, his afternoons reading in the shuttered hall, turning in early, the rainbow flicker of the television playing on in the darkness.

The afternoon before the day of the party they had cut a clearing close to the house, the helicopter bringing the first guests across the straits from the mainland, the loose shutters flapping like clapper-sticks, flurries of bright petals driven in over the marble floors and patios; the garden on that side of the house suddenly denied all colour.

But the morning of the party I woke with a clammy fever, and moped about all day construing single verses from my mother's books, and in the evening I stayed in with my father and watched the news in many languages which he trapped like migrant messenger birds in the webbed satellite-bowl he had installed on the lawn that had never taken, the sand showing through beneath.

But I had made a romance of her isolation. Sylvie was never elusive. Most afternoons she would come down on the back of the scooter with Anna to the bar in the old town where I had first found Shaman, sitting with the rest of the gang in her jeans and ravelled cardigan, pecking on the passed joints, not saying much, but listening to the talk of the evening to come and evenings spent and what might have been that summer as if it were all a play and she had arrived too late to be moved by what happened next.

When Anna answered for her, and she usually did, her face suddenly curdling, her pale lips stung and impliant, and for the rest of the evening that look of unsifting disenchantment I had already noted at the house; and from those empty years this expression only would survive in her.

Shaman's bike had broken down, and he would hitch in along the carretera from the marina, and sometimes he would bring a girl called Atlanta whose mother ran a boutique in one of the resorts beyond Bellamar, and she would always come dressed in skin-tight pedal-pushers and spangled halter-tops as if for a disco when it was the middle of the afternoon, and neither of the sisters would speak to her, and she was never accompanied to the Damas; her pressed thighs between the wrought-iron tables, the untanned nape of her neck as she looped up her platinum plaits, the flashing rhinestone clip in her lips like a silver fish thrown to a seal.

Later when the hour of the paseo had begun the plazita filling with courting couples and buzzing scooters, the tall boy with razored sideburns like inverted commas who I had seen that first night with Shaman lurching down on to the straw bench beside the table, not speaking or moving but slumped like a puppet whose strings have suddenly been cut.

Foley was older than Anna and Sylvie, and the only one to have a job, 'my gig', a cartoonist for an English-language newspaper based on the mainland, but he dressed the same, drainpipe jeans and a black leather jacket, a scarlet A in a circle on the shoulder-pads, and when he livened up after a cortado there was an antic energy in the abruptly wheeling and flaring Zippo that was like the dumb-show of a youthfulness which he had never truly owned, and could only mime now, from the outside.

And there was a melancholy in all this which the others did not see, for they too had confused energy for youth; it always seemed as if it was he who had accepted them, never the other way.

It was Foley who had turned the others on to sulphate, a habit he had picked up before dropping out of his first year at Magdalene, and though he may have had nothing further to impart he had retained the office of master-of-ceremonies.

Usually he would score down at El Paraíso, from one of the peeling bungalows with overgrown drives, but when he arrived he would take his time bringing out the wraps which were not offered to Sylvie, and they knew better than to hurry him.

In the penumbra of the shuttered bar, the cheek-glitter of the crystals; snorting the lines through dirty mille-pesetas from the upturned saucers, they would argue on about what to do that evening until it was too late to reach the resorts down the coast. The bar would be almost empty then, by the door the last macarras dithering over their beers, peering through the dusty orange trees to the scooters circling the plazita, hissing at Atlanta who would giggle and sit on her hands, but never at Sylvie whose presence they seemed hardly to notice.

Foley was still living with his vinolent mother who had retired from teaching at a North London nursing college to a water-mill she had renovated in the hills above Manilva; in the style of a rustic bodega the walls hung with painted water jugs and terracotta tiles, Sevillañas playing at all hours, a plague of geraniums at each door, the adobe outhouses worked into picturesque ruins, and he would not bike back until it was late and he was sure she was asleep.

When my silence had turned a shadow over the table, I would attempt to draw out details of his legendary decadence at school, and when this failed try to interest him in my old father's own drinking and waywardness, to forge an affinity over our mutual shame, but during the telling I would become lost in the sullen inflections of her lips, and forget my place.

There was much joshing from the others about introducing her to my father who had become a more vivid

37

presence at the table than myself to the extent that I was not encouraged to talk on any other subject.

Through my faltering accounts of his reclusive routines I had found a role within the gang I could play up to, and only Foley did not encourage my narrations, though at this stage I could hardly know whether his scrupulousness was intended to shelter or exclude.

We finished our Irish coffees with the lights up, the lantern-jawed barman stacking the stools, trundling his straw broom beneath our table; Foley leading the way through the unlit square, down towards the sea.

The building had once faced on to an esplanade above the beach, but since the supermarket and warehouse had been built all that side had been closed up. The empty terrace no longer saw the sun, the tessellated tiles cracked and overgrown, the peeling balustrade of anchor-and-triton motifs blind against the unpainted breeze-block walls, the interior still hung with photographs from the Fifties, dashing signatures across the corners, and above surrounded by broken bulbs the name of the bar in letters large enough to have been seen from the other side of the bay.

But people from the town rarely took this route to the beach now. As we descended I would walk behind Sylvie, but far enough back so she did not notice, and she would peer into the faded façade as if she had once lost something there, and yet she passed this place so many times it seemed there could be nothing she had not seen before.

Even through the rough-floored darkness in her sneakers and floppy cardigan she walked without ever entirely relaxing her poise, as if every step had been precisely choreographed long before, the rhythm of her slender calves and hips against her jeans along a course consecrated to some higher order of repetition.

Down on the beach Shaman always playing the same songs, snogging with Atlanta under the porch of the chiringuito boarded up until the summer, Anna and Foley dancing on the damp sand, the batteries slowly giving out, no moonshine on the wash, the lights of the gas rigs through the mist along the bay.

She would be still again, her knees bunched tight under her cardigan against the wind over the straits, and it was as if only Anna's gaze held her from springing out into the night.

When the wind dropped Foley would make a fire in the lee of the hut, and I would be careful not to sit beside her as we all gathered, a strange little gang we made huddled there over those guttering embers, coming down together at the furthest edge of that off-season resort which had never had much of a season even in the summer, and in a country we all had yet to understand, sharing little, as is the way with such bands to begin with, a rickety shelter from our separate futures, and from the emptiness of the coast, though each no doubt believing they had their own reason for being there, their own secret Sylvie, and none could have foreseen how the shelter of such passing amity could itself become that future which it seemed so blithely to suspend.

Through that winter after Sylvie had returned to school we would meet in the siesta-hour at the blind terrace behind the bar before driving into the pine hills.

Shaman had the shortest distance to come, from the Portakabin he had converted into a studio beside the unfinished block of timeshares on the carretera, but he would always arrive last after waiting for Atlanta, though if he had slept in the town on someone's floor I would find him when I arrived replacing with a stick of charcoal the details the rain had effaced from the wide-winged eagle sweeping over the faded Neptune-with-nereids which had once adorned the lower wall of the esplanade.

They made an odd couple, Shaman always in black,

strung-out and unshaven, his tousled hair and grave-digger pallor, Atlanta so pert and candy-bright in her satin baseball jacket and pedal-pushers, like a gift still to be unwrapped; she complained he had taken to roving the shoulders of the carretera in search of dead gulls and buzzards to sketch, and carried their smell on him, and so I arranged that he could wash in the pool cabin, though my father still refused to have him in the house.

My only design during those slow blank months to consolidate my position within the group, making myself of use, fronting cash for deals, driving when their motorbikes failed to the peeling bungalows beyond the breakwater.

It was already clear that the path to Sylvie ran through Anna, through Foley. By his absences, his doldrums, his wired exaltations, the other three kept time. He was the one to leave first, to whom promises were made, the dead centre of their illusions, and yet he was the only one who depended on me for nothing.

Through that winter after Sylvie had left we visited the places I would always think of first when I pictured my way back to the drifting almanac of those years, and I cherished them even then for what they could tell me of her life there before me.

On fine days, leaving the car at the end of the dirt-track below Castellar, walking up through the scrubland of junipers and wild rosemary and thyme to the rock-pool still too cold for swimming, everyone blinking in the hard light, leaning to keep their grip, their black leather jackets like giant beetles against the scree-face; Shaman scrambling ahead to wedge the bottles in the bed of the stream.

If there were fish we never saw any, and we would lie on the cool rocks with the Stranglers playing flat, the smoke of the fire trailing down between the umbrella pines on the breeze from the heights until the waters darkened over the straits.

I had been brought up on such country, driving each weekend with my father in his battered Plymouth up among the wadis and ruined kraks in search of some sheltered picnic spot he had first discovered with my mother, and it was not difficult to believe I knew the place already, and as I wandered through the scenery of her past I had the sense that she had unknowingly trespassed on to my own.

When the days became warmer we would drive beyond San Roque to a beach below the salt works which had no name; those were the years before the windsurfers, and when we had made our way down along the goat track to the strip of shingle we could no longer hear the rumble of the carretera behind the bluff, and there was a sudden aloneness which nothing could dispel, and all our prattle and shrieking only seemed to deepen, and we would sit and watch the grey Atlantic waves breaking on the outcrop, the sandpipers wading in the reed-rimmed shallows, the long dark tankers moving slow as shadows on a sun-dial out beyond the headland.

We never stayed there long. It was as if we had gone too far already, tagging a limit, and after Foley had hunkered down behind the bank to skin a porro for the road with Anna covering him against the wind and Atlanta had found her shoes again we would drive back behind the sluggish fruit lorries towards San Roque, the baroque glory of the darkening clouds above like a vast swab of candyfloss.

More often we would drive down the coast the other way to the resorts. We would aim to catch the second English-language performance at the cinema above the marina; the theatre of corrugated iron, like a small hangar, crabgrass growing between the wide steps, on either side of the portico faded posters in glass niches framed with a little roof and serrated borders like the roadside shrines in

41

the hills; the votive flowers at the feet of the plaster virgins wilted in the high sun over the sierra.

The lobby doubled as a bar, low-slung bamboo armchairs, sand-filled ashtray-troughs, through doubled velvet curtains the darkened auditorium, and it would be strange suddenly to be among so many English again, among the shuffling of high-waisted slacks and the cocktail-hour hubbub and the unemphatic semaphore of liver-spotted hands, among all those familiar colognes and smokes and scents, and this an Englishness petrified and distilled by long expatriation, and extinct to England like a grafted grape which thrives in foreign climes long after the original vines have been destroyed by pestilence.

Atlanta always pointing out Stuart Granger and Rod Laver and the other famous retirees from down the coast, the rest of the audience pretending not to notice, and I would be overcome by a curious pity for these old lions waiting alone by the bar to watch some unremarkable film among strangers.

When the performance was over we would walk down into the marina, in the narrow lanes Shaman and Foley gobbing on the tinted window-displays of marble tables, porcelain leopards, star-burst mirrors.

The bars on the front deserted; lone Arabs promenading with worry-beads, local couples on a night out. Over the dark straits the dim lights of the tankers still as the stars; along the shoreline through the mist the bleary neon like make-up run in the rain.

It would be quiet there in the quays; the water slopping against the hulls, the wind fretting in the stretched canvas, the dust of the desert on our gums, through the rigging and radar poles the avenue of moonshine which hung like a drop over each beach on the island, always the certainty of coming down to the same prospect, as if the coast was constantly shifting, and only the sea remained true.

Down on the quay we had reached a limit greater than that between sea and land, and this was not because we had come to the southernmost edge of the island as to the bottom of a vessel where the sediment settles over time, but rather out among those black waters with the lights of the farded promenade behind we had discovered the inseparable strangeness of each to the other.

Over the following weeks I would travel into their own secret island. Along goat tracks through the hills, on dirt-trails behind the silent urbanisations, through dried viaducts under the carretera; along the shingle-line below the empty summer villas.

Always avoiding the carretera; the policía along the coastal autovia.

I followed the dust clouds of their bikes through sandblown ravines and high dunes down to the hidden beaches; a rough arc of flaring torches, the sheen of chrome and smooth leather; against the tall speaker, Anna a star-splayed Andromeda chained to her cliff; bright sarongs fluttering like pennants in the wind across the straits.

The boys dancing on the sand as if walking in honey, hands pulling at the air like a crew of sailors hoisting some vast invisible sail.

All night we drove through the dilapidated cortijo resorts searching for dealers and parties.

When we returned at dawn to the valley Sylvie was never at the house, her appearances erratic and intermittent, her expensive new tailored suits like fancy dress among the macarras and surfers in the back-yards of the bungalows.

One afternoon she came with us to the Divina Pastora tenements below the stadium in Bellamar; across the waste-land under the porch the old woman sewing on her straw stool, three times waving her arm to the sky as if she were accustomed to conversing only with those who did not understand her; the husband gnarled and brown as a walnut, lifting his straw hat, his bald pate white as eggshell.

Under lacrimose madonnas on the unplastered walls the son brings the scales and wraps out over the plastic table with a parasol hole; she looks at her watch, and without waving hurries down the unlighted stairs. Foley had told me of a sugar-daddy at the other end of the coast who did not like to be kept waiting.

Through the window I peer after her along the unpaved street, the niños running circles around her, calling 'puta' 'putana', her hair like syrup pouring into the night; beyond the lower tenements, massed aerials like dead bouquets.

As summer comes again we drive with Shaman to a village far up in the hills abandoned after the wells had dried, the road precipitous and blocked by landfalls, the remaining adobe shacks occupied by bead-selling hippies and macarras hiding out from dealers on the coast.

At the end of the trail we leave the car, and walk along the stream beds and rank pools high into the forest of cork trees, the white ash-tracks of the wildfires leading between hollowed holm oaks and thorn bushes strung with dead lizards and cicadas, above the flat rocks the shadows of circling shrikes and across the straits from the parched mountains the teeming flights of cattle-birds and short-toe eagles, their outstretched wings long and still as the wide-spanned gliders launched from the bell-tower at school, the eaglets in their lower spirals landing clumsily like our discarded shirts.

We pass a dead goat under a swarm of hook-bills nosing deep into the carcass, above on the branches the silhouettes of the preening vultures, and as we come down to the village at nightfall we hear the call of the wood-owl sharp as the umpire's final whistle, in the lower groves the cork-harvesters stacking the peeled bark on to the donkey trains, through the darkening trees the wide-screen sunset with its lakes of molten ochre and vermilion, the last ragged clouds like sheep coming in to be watered.

The night I heard the bell I thought it must be Shaman up from the poolhouse. I ran across the hall; I did not want the ringing to wake my father for then he would pace the corridors all night and I would not sleep.

Below the steps she was standing in her old cardigan and jeans; out on the unlit drive beyond the satellite-dish, the shadowed curve of a new convertible.

Under the oak table she squatted and opened the wrap, the crystals glimmering in the flicker from the television my father never turned off.

On the walls, no paintings, no mirrors. I brought her the olive-wood casket, and as she turns it over a sound like the sifting of dry bones.

We sat in the rainbow arc of the television; the bob of the announcer the high blonde of goldfish scales; the white domes of the Invalides, giant eggs about to hatch into something indescribable.

I went for cigarettes into the bedroom, and she followed, and when I kissed her she pulled her head away, and turned her back, her buttocks pressing lightly against my crotch.

Her hands lazy over her thighs as if over a sleeping pet, her jeans catching at the knees so it hurt pushing in, the sudden outward thrust of her lips like a child miming a fish.

And afterwards she said nothing, and crouched against the wall, but grasping my hand so tight as if on the edge of a precipice, and when I woke to the first light over the beach through the undrawn curtains she was gone.

1983, 1984

I

Our earliest memories live on within us and resonate late into our unforeseen endings, a buried hearth whose warmth will never entirely be dissipated by the wide arc of the years.

He remembers one Christmas when of course there were many. The annual rituals of childhood with their cherished repetitions lying lightly one on the other until pressed by the weight of the years into a single enduring form.

His elder brother Anton was guardian of the manger, the olive-wood figures stored in the lowest drawer of his wardrobe. He longs to hold again the Three Wise Men riding on their camels, smaller and more delicate than the other figures for from the perspective of the manger they are still crossing the desert; he never finds the drawer unlocked.

Nine days before Christmas the stage for the manger laid above the dresser in the kitchen where he could not reach; lentils and grain spread on the large tray, watered until the green shoots sprout.

The shoots clipped with scissors until they are short and even, a miniature lawn, the tray placed in the dark corner under the bokhara tapestries, surrounded with flickering candles.

He sits for hours before the grotto, his legs numb. He reaches in to adjust the position of one of his beloved kings

49

but so fractionally his intervention will never be noticed. Melchior, with his hamper of gold, Gaspar the black king, his turban like a painted snail.

When Mama suffers in the cold Jerusalem winters they take a carossa to Jericho, and return with oranges from the family bayyara; or wine and brandy from Richon-le-Zion, the Jewish vineyard on the Jaffa Road.

When there is ice on the well, and frost on the cyclamen beds, Mama resorts to the cassat. He watches his sister Anastasia apply the glass jars to her back, the thin strips of paper still burning within. When the jars are removed they make a round plopping like a bottle being uncorked; the skin beneath flushed a lurid purple.

After the applications, an alchohol rub, and she retires to bed.

By April the cold has passed. He remembers the Easter cakes, a hollow corona wide as the palm of a hand. The coarse smeed flour stuffed with dates, almonds, walnuts, pine-kernels; the edges decorated in a pinched pattern with hot tongs.

He shadows the large trays lined with doilies from beneath, a cat chasing pigeons.

In Holy Week all the children in the neighbourhood take to the streets for the egg-cracking competition. Only one egg out of hundreds will emerge victorious; the game like conkers, but played with hard-boiled eggs, dyed and painted in bright colours.

The defender holds his egg upright in his fist, exposing the flatter end; his opponent hammers with a pecking motion until one of the shells cracks.

And when the rounds of the day are over they come inside to the broth of pine-kernels and meatballs stuffed with thyme and basil, its magical taste, like that of the cakes, seasoned by the knowledge it will not be enjoyed again for another whole year.

That Thursday morning the barber trims Baba's beard. Mama checks that his feet are scrubbed, his nails clipped. In the afternoon the family joins the crowd outside the Holy Sepulchre, in the courtyard a raised platform where Baba sits among the twelve clergymen. The Patriarch Damianos kneels and washes their feet as Christ had washed the feet of his disciples.

In the doorways, sleeping Russian peasants, jurd hares in their fur coats; wealthier pilgrims bringing gifts for Baba: embroidered guilloche shawls, silver eggs etched with elaborate bouquets and holy vignettes.

Like bats in a cave the Patriarch and his followers fluttering barefoot in their long robes under the low vaults from one dark corner to another, the front rows of the faithful peering forward, the iron-toed boots over the flagstones like knives being sharpened, the intoning of prayers under their breath like the moan of the first sand wind through the hills, suddenly in the darkness a faint flicker, the murmur of prayers rising to an ecstatic chant as the fire passes from torch to taper to lantern until the whole square is burning with a thousand flames; the holy fires carried flickering back by package boat from Jaffa through the Dardanelles to the Black Sea, across the Volga and the Ural Mountains to the furthest reaches of Siberia, and those pilgrims who died on the journey were blessed for their souls ascended directly to heaven, and he believed then that all such faraway places were dark and cold wastes and the precious fire their single hope of light and warmth for the year to come.

Like so many pieces of putty squeezed together until they become indivisible these Easters of his childhood compressed by time into this single passage. They have the same irreducible essence as the house, its chiselled blocks of grey Jerusalem stone, the old paved verandah facing eastwards to the walled city.

On this verandah Baba sits in the afternoons in his slippers drinking Turkish coffee, smoking the oval cigarettes of which Mama disapproves. Here he reads to the blind theologians, receives his visitors, Greek monks, Copts, Armenians, Syriacs, Sunni Sheikhs; questions of theology and astronomy, undertones of conspiracy; the warmed cedar of their worry-beads, a scent he would recognise years later in the resorts of the Lebanon mountains.

Baba's skin pale as the parchment on which he practises his calligraphy, the Indian-ink blotted with sand carried on the winds through the tamarisk hedges; his pens carved from the thin reeds down on the wadi-banks under the hill.

In winter his pallor accentuated by the long muslin gown and black pleated cap; in summer by the cream robes and tall cylindrical hat he wears into the old town.

Baba never took part in the social life of the house, the tea-parties, the musical evenings organised by Anton and Mama, all the guests bowing on the path under the verandah to receive his blessing before entering the shade of the vine trellises.

Beyond the covered verandah, an old well with rope grooves over the sandstone through long usage. Hen houses, a ruined windmill, under the stone wall to the gates the cyclamen beds in which the twins bury their half-piastres believing they will take root and grow into money trees.

He calls into the well, and flees the echoes into the hills; under the cover of wild figs he listens for the calls of the masons who come up the path from St Stephen's Gate to quarry the hard grey rock from which the house and all the city are built.

On this path Baba walks each morning to his church at the Holy Sepulchre, down through the steep soukh, market-traders and hamals touching the hem of his robes, basket-boys bearing water-melons and coussa back through the lanes to the house.

Wherever he wanders among the seven hills the driver will stop his bus, Baba always politely declining the ride, walking on through the heat of the day to the quarters of his parishioners.

On the evening verandah he awaits the return of his father; the old man holding up a closed fist; he struggles to prise the hand open finger by finger to reach the petits fours and stuffed dates saved from parish visits; always they emerge miraculously unscathed.

Inside the guests have already arrived; in the summer, sherbert, citron pressé cooled with shavings from the ice-house; marrons glacés; sugared orange-peel, dates stuffed with blanched almonds. The old lady empties the sediment from her coffee cup, and reads the portents of a long sea voyage.

The twins watching from the door, a visiting daughter or Anastasia singing accompanied by Anton on the piano, never dancing; afterwards the magical gramophone, the conical speaker like the loud-hailers of the barkers at the Hungarian circus outside the walls where they were forbidden to go.

The black box is inhabited by the midget Magyar. The twins feed him grains of rice and lentils; when he no longer sings Anton tells them they have poisoned him. Did they not know that Magyars eat only cabbages and horse flesh?

The brass charcoal brazier, the only source of heating in the house; under the pale glow of kerosene lamps the dark swirls of the bokharas and kelims; a map of her heart, says Anastasia.

In summer these rugs are beaten, rolled, bound with twine, stacked in the attics. He hears a maid has been sent to fetch Nili, he goes ahead unobserved and hides in a hollow pillar; over the cedar beams the long shadows from her candle. She approaches, he rises slowly with a low growling, the girl drops her candle, fleeing, screeching

53

'Ghul, ghul'. The origins of the apparition are explained; still she refuses ever to return to the attics.

From the attic window he looks down to the yard outside the kitchens, a mountain of stuffing from all the mattresses, cushions, pillows, the mnajed drawing the cotton through his three-stringed harp like spun sugar; that night he floats on the back of a cloud high over the golden dome.

From the upper floor they watch the Turkish soldiers felling the neighbouring orchards; the wood as fuel for the trains to Damascus and Aleppo, the unripe fruit to the camps beyond the olive orchards; from the houses the soldiers bring pots, pans, candlesticks, the mule trains swaying slowly in the lanes as if invisible winds blow against them.

'Those men the Turks took we never saw again.' They are under the age of conscription, but the three brothers are hidden inside tall linen baskets; over the hills, distant artillery crumps, like carpets being beaten out over the balconies in the first weeks of autumn.

In the early mornings they wake to the hoarse cries of the fruit-sellers, the catcalls of drunken soldiers. From his drawer Baba unwraps the virgin rolls of gold lira, the tradesmen wait in the hall. Below all day in the garden the ataals heaving sacks and crates into the cellars – beans, wheat, flour, almonds, coffee; tins of olives, sardines; of honey and jam.

Each time they lift their loads, they recite lines from the Qur'ān.

Believers, eat of the wholesome things and give thanks to God.

In the name of the compassionate, the merciful, remember he who fed them in the days of famine and sheltered them from all peril.

At last it was as if they were embarking on that long and arduous sea voyage the old lady had predicted.

Along the shoreline through the mist the bleary neon of the marina bars, over the waste-lots of the deserted ferias garlands of fairy lights strung in the plane trees. Out on the black straits the faint lights of the tankers still as the moon.

I drive back between the peeling bungalows where we had gone together the previous winter, but most have been abandoned, boarded-up; over the empty yards the chuchos barking.

Down to the beaches the turnings are blocked by barbed wire, giant hoardings with bright paintings of unbuilt developments, the bays floating with dust and debris from the diggers.

In the bar on the little square and in the marinas I had searched for the girls and Shaman, the macarras turning away, as if I were a policeman; the lantern-jawed barman said he had not seen the Ingleses for many months.

Where the Portakabin studio had been, a maze of time-share pueblos, crazy-paving paths leading over new-laid grass to azure-tiled kidney pools, shells of unfinished cortijos across the old trail through the umbrella pines to the tennis club, through the poured concrete the girder-twists like the masts of sunken wrecks.

The landscape constantly shifting, drops in a studio lot, the hills suddenly planted with grand white villas, classical ambulatories, bordello-rococo poolhouses, all the follies and caprices on the walls of the house in the valley designs for monuments as yet invisible.

Through the pine ridges, glimpses of tall grey walls, a golden dome. An old priest walking in the heat of the noon, a carossa listing under crates of oranges.

The dome an unturned concrete bowl, a new mosque for the summer princes and arms-dealers.

That Christmas I had returned from my first term at York University; Palgrave and the fops had decamped to Oxford,

Gervase Webb to Savile Row; we would not meet again for several years.

I had rented the converted stable of a large house on the lower rim of the moors, with a view across paddocks through oak trees and poplars to the former gamekeeper's cottage in the lee of the bracken-covered combe rented to a couple my landlady described as 'the inverts'.

The village had no shops, only the farm-produce store which sold the vegetables and free-range eggs on which I subsisted, and one afternoon from the gravel parking-lot I had looked down into the garden of the cottage, there under the hedge of scarlet haws the dapper figure of Nick Reaper strolling in a fisherman's jersey and a tartan scarf through the fallen chestnut leaves, beyond on the edge of the field a row of skeletal poplars against the autumn dusk; his hair already greying at the temples, his kicking at the leaves violent, impatient, his restlessness like that of an emigrant still waiting on a final permit.

He was in his last year at the university, and rarely ventured out to the campus. For weeks he would be away in London, returning with crates of Bollinger, new suits, velvet-collared overcoats from Gieves. I had forgotten he was a scholarship boy, and so at the time did not question this extravagance.

Sometimes I would be invited to the cottage for dinner, a pot-au-feu cooking over a slow fire, upstairs in a perfumed bath his long-fringed Etonian companion reclining with a cheroot and Belgian chocolates, peering out at the moors as if they were a watercolour he had not quite tired of yet.

Reaper would never talk about his trips to London, nor about his schooldays, though he affected to remember me, but it was at one of these dinners he told me he had seen Foley in a squat in Kilburn, lying in bed all day, whacking up heroin; at weekends selling his cartoons to tourists at Camden Lock.

My first afternoon back on the island I had driven to the house in the valley. The gates open, the sunlight flickering on the filled pool, a workman standing over the water with a long pole like a gondolier.

Under the awning of the poolhouse, Monica hidden behind her easel; her muscular trainer reposing over the sun-lounger; beside him she seemed both pliable and powerful, like a mistress with a large dog.

On the canvas, a sketch of the house: the date palms, the blue shutters, the tower. She wanted a record of the place, she said; it would be sold in the divorce.

She told me the girls would not want to keep the house up, Anna had grown her hair and was modelling, her new boyfriend Nick Reaper had come into money, Bloom had arranged it all, little Sylvie who he had never thought of as his own, she had been looked after as part of a deal with Don Luis who used to own half of Bellamar before he sold to the developers and retreated to his hunting lodge in the cork forests at the far end of the coast.

She spoke lightly, as if giving instructions for the laying of place-mats; she offered me a Bloody Mary, but I did not stay, nor once looked back at the house as I drove through the olive terraces into the hills.

It was a fortnight before Sylvie rang, and we agreed to meet at a restaurant in Bellamar.

La Virginia was the oldest urbanisation to the west of the city, a dusty quadrangle of shuttered villas and peeling eucalyptus trees cut off from the beach by the carretera and high-rise condominiums which had stolen the views down to the sea; the tables of the pretentious little restaurant around the moss-floored plazita with its trickling majolica fountain, the other diners retired expatriates, the elderly women all with their hair up, their jewellery flickering like fireflies as they turned to peer at each other across the candlelit patio.

She was already there in the same old jeans and cardigan, and though I had arrived early she complained I had kept her waiting, played with her food and drank too much, giggling at the old couples with her hand held over her mouth.

Sweating in my corduroys, I followed her to the covered shrine over the square; we leant on the rickety balustrade and looked down over the dim contours of the crucifixion, her lips dry and chapped, her hands gently stroking my crotch until she bent and sucked with a casual brusqueness as if from a drinking fountain.

Her lips glistening, she took a candle from the rack, knelt on the mildewed boards, guiding my thrusts, her teeth piercing my lower lip as she stiffened, and we clung together in the darkness without speaking as one by one the large saloons of the diners pulled out from the square and down to the hum of the carretera.

II

The works of a novelist read in quick succession merge into a single compound tale. When we return to the individual books, the surprising outcomes and omissions betraying our memories.

Like the Easters of my father's childhood all that remains of those journeys we took together when I returned for the holidays are these few brief sequences, the arbitrarily surviving footage of lost film.

We would drive from the coast into the hinterland, the narrow lanes of the obrero barrios above San Roque and Bellamar slow with Mobylettes and burros and tricycletas laden with panniers of olives and grapes from the hills, through the rainbow haze of the diesel fumes along dusty avenues of plane and eucalyptus, through olive terraces and sunflower fields to the parched air of the lower ranges.

Over the rough cambers of the high passes, sheer drops of white rock to the charred skeletons of fallen cars; on the hairpin corners, stucco shrines; far below the workers among the flooded caissons of the new autovia.

Our first tintos of the day at the wayside tapaterias, your bare legs coiled on the straw stool, flies circling the glass counter; the earthenware pots of brackish pulpo, sardines, croquettas.

In the inland pueblos beyond the sierra you stand at the

windows of the old-fashioned patisserias. Almond fingers, nougat, almond cake, apricot tartlet, flan a la religiosa, charlotte of pears; elaborately painted tins of turrón. Your slight reflection, an allegory of famine.

On the hills above the pueblos, enclosed cemeteries under cypress trees. We walked between walls of tombs like giant chests of drawers. You always wanted to see the oldest grave, and the newest. You wore the wilted flowers in your hair. Over the filigree gold script on the cool black marble you spread yourself like an old cat, still as an effigy.

We crossed the plains beyond the last sierra. On the outcrops, high black silhouettes, the Sandeman, the Black Bull. Under the rusting scaffolding dumps of broken cookers, sinks, ripped mattresses; the stench of urine and perished rubber.

You pulled me down, we rolled in the dust like hogs, stones and rough grasses scratching our backs and legs.

You told me, 'Love consists of being silly beasts together,' all day I would wonder where you had heard this line.

You led me down from the road through abandoned terraces to rock-pools along the stream beds, under the slow green current, your sudden flexings lithe as a water rat.

And always as you dried yourself on the sun-baked rocks in the shade of the grove the wide-brimmed straw hats of the silent campesinos.

We came down into the towns at the hour of the paseo. In the squares of linden trees the courting couples and widows with fans walking between the kiosks selling bomboms and bright pops.

In the lobby of the posada the taciturn concierge took our single case, and we followed up the cool of the stairs to the room; your damp bare feet on the tiles like a child being slapped.

The twin beds with studded leather headboards, the

rough oak settle and bedside table, your dirty nails strumming the notched edges. Out beyond the window the night pulled down like a curtain over the plains.

You repeat yourself like a song. I wake to the glow of your first Camel, already noon, a lattice of white light through the thin curtains. The floor-tiles shimmering with suds from the flooded shower, your haunches pale as a heron at dusk.

She does not look out at the view. Down on the empty terrace she drinks her silted cortado; the napkins still folded over the croissants and bollos in the straw basket.

She waits in the convertible, smokes her second cigarette, her hair drying in the parched winds as we drive on without a map.

We return by the old roads. The bustling little plazitas in the small towns welcoming us as if we had lived there all our lives.

'There are those women who when you are with them make you feel there has never been anyone before, nor will there ever be anyone afterwards.'

On the few cultivated strips under the lee of the ridges, the lone campesinos as if trespassers over the pure glare of those barren heights.

In the late afternoon we came down again into the humid terraces and pine hills of the coast. We crept into deserted villas, through the high hedges of wisteria, the molten sunset beyond the straits like a cheap postcard.

Titles are wild indeterminate promises which may never be fulfilled. We read for we are compelled to be betrayed. In the shuttered darkness you run your bruised fingers along the spines.

You open the books with the violence of a child unwrapping a gift she has already received. Pressed flowers, sticking-plasters, Palm-Sunday crosses, hairclips; you garner fetishes for secret spellings; these houses belong to the friends of your father.

You swig from the bottles of spirits in the drinks cabinets, their labels illegible in the half-light, books perching like birds on your little hand before fluttering into unseen corners.

You look up a word in the dictionary when you already know the meaning. It takes an age for you have never learnt your alphabet.

'How could I find so many rare and beautiful words if I did not wander first?

'How would I have discovered so much if I had always found my way home?'

And yet through all those precious days and nights you said no other words that I remember.

You wanted to be fucked in the afternoons when the rest of the coast slept. In frowsty poolhouses, on cold floors, on the dustsheets in the shuttered halls; a snail, trailing your glissade over my nakedness.

Translating from our island dialect you told me a girl was like a fire in the wind who must be kindled with care before she will hiss and spit and roar, but at first we were always rough with each other.

You rode and rubbed until we were both sore and dry, a punitive rigour; you were scrubbing a wound until the blood could not be staunched.

You disavowed all tenderness, but always in your eyes the lights of a lonely house; when it was over only a fraternal clasp, like friends after a wrestle.

You needed to hear words of abuse, only then would you lie shuddering on my stomach; you were never satisfied with the stock epithets, you needed to hear other names.

'Imagine you were being unfaithful to me – with a putilla, with Anna, a putana – call me by her name.'

And as you took a secret pride in your depravity, so your clothes became ever more modest; skirts and tops no longer clinging, undefining jeans, the denim faded, coarse; verisma make-up.

Not a disguise, nor the the frisson of faked primness, only the simple shame of those who have been taught they will never be loved.

In those first dank weeks in Yorkshire you would not leave the bedroom. I had turned up the storage-heaters, you said the house was as cold as the bottom of a well.

From the window you threw down toast and biscuits from the bedside table to the peacocks we had stolen from the grounds of Castle Howard. At night their terrible howling kept us awake. During the day we could not see them for the tall nettles and moor mists.

I would return from my seminar on campus to find smeared reliefs on the wainscoting, dark menstrual impastos. Crude eagles, trail motorcycles, date palms; like ancient cave-paintings. I did not wipe them away.

In the winter the castle was closed to visitors, but I knew a back route into the lower gardens, the road passing the farm shop above Reaper's cottage, now occupied by more conventional students, a camper-van in the drive, boys in bright jerseys chopping wood in the hollow where I had first watched him pace among the fallen chestnut leaves the previous autumn.

Between livid green fields and copses of oak and poplar to the first low wall, the tip of the distant obelisk rising through the arch of the rusticated gate like a gunsight, the track leading to a bridge over a bramble-covered crater where water had never flowed; above on the steep hill the rotunda of the mausoleum; the Portland parapets at the base of the columns charred from the fires of the students who came at dawn in the season to pick magic mushrooms on the banks.

From the hill we wandered down through chicken-wire

fences into the lower gardens. We followed the gravel paths between dry fountains and untrimmed topiary, on its long plinth the stone boar under a web of scaffolding; a second wooded hill to the east where you refused to climb, on the crest the temple dedicated to the Four Winds.

I told you that three years before they had filmed Brideshead Revisited in these grounds, you pretended never to have heard of it. I had come to Yorkshire to escape the fops, and was fated to wander the landscape of their fantasies.

One afternoon I returned from my seminar to find the bedroom empty. A trail of hanging smoke through the empty rooms and out along a loop of crushed nettles doubling back into the house. Your jeans and T-shirts still lying where they had fallen, but the leather grip-bag you had never unpacked no longer beside the bed. They had bloomed like tropical flowers in my austere bathroom, now the bright cream-pots and make-up pouches were gone.

Under the pillows, on my desk, on the mirror above the fire. I looked for the note, but found nothing.

In those remaining weeks of the term, the smears slowly flaking from the walls; the room heavy with your inner scents.

Above the ribbon developments of condominiums and obrero tenements to the east of Bellamar, the van straining on the climb, over the mirror the shuddering juju-beads of the rosary; up through the avocado and zucchini terraces, through the cork forests left wild for hunting; the entrance to the lodge an arch of glazed majolica between fallow terracotta urns.

I left the van at the bottom of the drive, and walked up under the cover of the hibiscus, through the palmettos under the long white portico of the finca; vine trellises over the sallow rose of the roman-tile gables.

The verandahs empty, the chairs and tables stacked against the troughs, the shaded walkway coming out above a sand-floored cortijo, the whitewashed adobe walls hung with bunting and crêpe streamers; over the sand between large kegs and barrels, the jagged tracks of a jaleo, dried petals of white and pink confetti.

The old gardener must have presumed I was a guest who had come on the wrong day, and with an overbearing deference conducted me through the mosaic-walled patio and the cool of the panelled hall to a large oak dresser.

Under the Bakelite telephone, a stack of cream-framed Polaroids, collapsed like a deck of cards. The horse caparisoned with the traditional bells and painted halters, Sylvie side-saddle in her billowing organza gown, the old hidalgo looking out from under the brim of his black hat over the forests to the saw-teeth of the high sierra; I could not see his eyes.

The voice of the gardener was soft, reverential, as if the guardian of a remote shrine to which only the most devout ventured.

The Don and the nueva Doña would not be returning from their honeymoon in Granada until the end of the month – o sea más tarde, señor; his unknowing cruelty so exquisite that holding my hand over my eyes I reached into my pocket for a tip.

In those weeks of waiting in the villa I did not go up to the tennis club, or walk down the beach to the marina bars.

I stayed within range of the one telephone in the corridor. In the house there was nothing to read; my schoolboy German was not strong enough to translate the old volumes of Schiller and Heine in my room. I stood in the drained pool, and rallied with myself against the higher end.

In the late afternoon I came up into the darkening hall, the bare walls swimming with television flicker, the sound down, my father invisible behind the armchair, a faint clicking of ice, the curtains masking the fading contours of the deserted links and the glow of the rubbish fires under the breakwater.

I crossed the floor silently behind his corner, but he was always already speaking, and I did not know if he was talking to himself, or began only when I had entered like the spotlight over the drive which when the invisible beam was broken illuminated not the steps to the porch but where the wind had driven the sand over the dying lawns.

III

Over the estuary the rising stork flights.

Paper flags and white banners waving in unison, a great fanfare of pipes and drums down the Jaffa Road.

He has never seen such a crowd before, never imagined his quiet city contained such multitudes.

Over the cobbles the percussion of hooves; through the gates, Generals Allenby and Walker riding ahead of the troops.

Anton lifting him on his shoulders; he sees only the sweat-black backs of the fellahin.

From the ruined windmill he chases the clouds of dust across the road, never sighting a motor car.

In the years following the arrival of the British so many changes.

In the house, kerosene lamps replaced by electric bulbs, the leather cushions charred from being thrown up against the flaring cables.

He was never allowed to touch the black cups of the telephone. When the Sheikh visited to speak to the governor of Jaffa, he thought it discourteous not to pour his coffee down the mouthpiece.

In the stalls outside St Stephen's Gate, new delicacies appearing, tinned bully-beef, Nestlé's milk chocolate. Over the years he collects every token, only the Golden Nest eludes him.

On the wasteground where there had been the Hungarian circus and occasional hangings, of which postcards would be circulated, the crowds now gather in a tin hut to watch a magic silver window.

On the street each year, the veil becoming more transparent until it vanishes altogether only to reappear on the faces of the fashionable women of Paris and London, their monochrome shades flickering on the magic window and sealed between the pages of Anastasia's scrapbook like the dead leaves of some exotic shrub.

From the kitchen door the twins watch as Mama and Anastasia wash and set their hair, the maid fetching water warmed over the brazier in a deep porcelain jug, her chapped hands lathering the hard unscented soap brought to the house by the the street-shabb from Nablus; the same bar used for washing clothes and dishes.

Like the keys of the piano the stockings of the women are black or white, but one day Frau Geli gives the music lesson in hosiery the colour of flesh, the twins staying awake all the night, praying Mama and Anastasia never succumb to such a scandalous fashion.

Her hair, the dark golden syrup poured over the hot crusts of kenafeh and the transparent millefeuilles of baclava, loose strands falling over her starched cream collar; they take turns to lick, so gently she feels nothing.

In his office in the sandstone government building the British have built above the city, Anton plays cards all day with his friends, smokes cigarillos, signs the papers the secretaries bring through without reading them.

With his new salary he buys a Model T Ford from the new showroom on the Jaffa Road. Every evening under the tasselled lamp he reads the User's Manual. He intones the lines like scripture. 'A few drops of oil may be added to the petrol to improve the running of the engine.'

In the night the twins creep down to feed the thin horses;

they pour an entire can of oil through the funnel into the petrol-nozzle. The following morning they wake to find Anton sweating over the crank-handle.

When the car has been repaired they drive for the day to Jaffa. The Armenian chauffeur covers the tyres in old spilt tubes against the nails and sharp stones, in the Wadi-of-the-Robber they drink lemon gazeuse at the roadside barakiat, driving on through the barren hills of gorse and prickly pear, far below a plain of orange trees and vines, and the glistening oil-slick of the sea.

When Baba had been a young man the journey by carossa had taken two whole days, an overnight stop at the Wadi al-Haramie; the legendary robber would stagger along the side of the road under the weight of an enormous sack until a passing traveller took pity and stopped their carriage, he would draw out a large cudgel from the sack and rob them of all they had; he was later hung by the Turks in the wasteground where the cinema had been built.

Anton never learnt to drive. Early every morning he would practise with his Armenian chauffeur along the deserted avenues of Mamilla. Each month he ran over a fellah carrying brushwood down from the hills, the clearance of the axle so high they always escaped unscathed.

On Sundays Anton locks himself in his room with his violin teacher, Herr Walter, Geli's husband; the twins place a ladder outside the door, but through the stained-glass fanlight they can never see the strange device which emits the wailing they cannot escape.

At the beginning of each term, Baba taking the twins to pray at his church beside the Holy Sepulchre, along the vaulted walls the icons blurred by the kisses of the centuries.

By St Stephen's Gate, through which every tourist passed into the old city, the bright blue letters over the American Colony Stores: SOUVENIRS. In the windows racks of olive-wood caskets, silver jewellery, brass salvers, embroidered kaftans from the neighbouring villages.

Under the bustling entrance of the soukh, the new office of Thomas Cook; the ruddy-faced Franks waiting in their tropical suits and sun-hats for the charabancs climbing through the hills to the white-tent encampments at Bethlehem, Jericho, to the level shore of the Dead Sea.

Opposite the furrows where the foundations are being dug for the King David Hotel, an elegant house with many balconies of grey stone; on the walls of the diwan, the swirls of hanging rugs convoluted as the smoke of a sistra; a silent parrot in a rusting cage, a maid sweeping geranium petals; as if time had healed itself in that one walk reprieved indefinitely from the sudden evictions of history.

St Georges was run along the lines of an English public school. Cold showers every morning, exercises before classes, on Saturday evenings as a privilege hot showers supervised by the prefects.

Each morning vespers in the Anglican cathedral, the shoes of the choristers snatched at the west door, their white socks protruding from under their smocks down the long aisle.

Turf was impossible to cultivate in Jerusalem. Cricket played on a dirt pitch, a wicket made from coconut matting; their hands numb from canings, the juniors on punishment-duty picking every stone from the weave, raking the sand with their eyelashes.

Good behaviour was rewarded with chocolate éclairs from the tuck-shop, excursions by donkey to the spring at Ein Fara.

The boys sewing bags in the lining of their sports jackets to smuggle out the stews and glutinous porridge from the refectory; each morning, on his way to the government building, Anton dropping gingham wraps of sambusek and lahmeh ajeen in the alley beside the dormitory block.

On market days the twins go hungry. Janitors are posted at the gates to regulate the boisterous fellahin who walk the twelve miles from Ramallah; on their heads straw panniers of olives, oranges, coussa; from the windows the boys cast down fishing lines, hoist up fruit from the open baskets.

The peasant women so hardy that if one gives birth on the road she cuts the umbilical cord with a sharp stone, and continues on her way.

Mama said the fogs which covered the island were so dense a man could not see his own feet. Inglisi had dark-adapted eyes, but travellers were led by false lights into marshes, and those who returned had forgotten their own tongue, and strutted along the Jaffa Road in tweed jackets puffing on briar pipes.

When the twins were of age to go to university Mama pleaded they be given quarters in the sandstone serail above the city, but Anton assauged her fears by ordering from Damascus two thick brocade dressing-gowns with velvet collars, two full-length sheepskin overcoats.

Overlooking the quay in the bar of the Messagerie Maritime, the twins celebrated their new freedom by sharing their first packet of cigarettes: Craven A, cork-tipped.

The stench of the half-cured hides pervading the cabins, the compartments of the trains from Marseilles to Cambridge, their room at the University Arms.

Not knowing which college to choose, the boys consulting the retired general who loitered gallantly about the lobby in a long coat with shining brass buttons; when the hall porter advised Queens', 'for it is at least four hundred years older than the other houses with vacancies', the twins taking him for a prankster; at home antiquity was synonymous with dilapidation, this prejudice inscribed in the word antika: that which is old, to be cast away.

The only Inglisi the twins had ever met outside school was

71

the fat man called Chesterton; he had spent many afternoons on the narghile verandah with Baba, and afterwards had written a book about their city.

It was to his mock-Tudor house in Beaconsfield that they called for a letter of recommendation to the venerable Dr Venn; through the conservatory windows the flourishing cyclamen beds grown from the bulbs Mama had given to the wife of the writer; he remembers the tidy borders along the grey-stone wall where as a boy he had planted half-piastres in the hope they would grow into money trees; though he had rooted like a hog in the damp earth he had never found one coin again.

On the ink-stained table, a great spread of crumpets, buns, jam tarts, the girth of the writer as he emerges from his study so round and inflated it seems at any moment he will rise into the sky like a helium balloon; that week two dirigibles had been released into the stratosphere to collect data on conditions there.

The spotted bow-tie of his dapper companion Belloc similar to those of the barkers on the wasteground under the walls by the Hungarian Circus, this manzul clown denouncing the balloon expeditions as a 'discordant meddling in the music of the spheres'; out of politeness the twins laughing uproariously.

The writer tells the boys his family are estate-agents, with pretensions above their class; as a boy he would be caned if he was ever heard dropping an 'h' even in jest; in the streets of Cambridge the twins never see men carrying 'h's, those on the signs above the shops seeming no more or less secure than the other letters.

At the barber's Pascal informing his brother with the air of an initiate that for a further sixpence he can request musical accompaniment while in the chair; not until he smelt the burning did he see the entry on the roll of extras: Singeing: 6d.

During their vacations the twins revised for their law exams at a residential hotel a few miles south of Beaconsfield. He takes his cane and goes down for a short walk before dinner, and as he strolls through the lobby a frail old lady smiles, asking with a casual air if he is about to take his constitutional.

He returns to the hotel sweating and shaking, from now on he will have to be on his guard, his inner motives and thoughts are transparent to the most casual onlooker.

Jamila had always said the Inglisi were conjurers of afreets and djinns, spending their nights alone among the stones of the dead, the villagers judging their pale skin a sign of leprosy, and fleeing into the baladi.

No single hill lay between the city and the steppes of Siberia, their sheepskin coats little protection against the harsh winds.

The twins did not excel at games, they rowed in the third boat in the bump races, the Cam being too narrow to accommodate races abreast, and only just avoided the disgrace of a bumping from the Newnham boat; the footballs were too slippery and heavy to suit their game.

They bought an HMV gramophone, in the form of a suitcase, with the speaker in the lid; it required continual winding, and regular replenishment with new needles. On more clement afternoons they took this contraption out on a punt, always playing Roy Fox and his Big Band; they had no other records. None of their friends could believe they had never learnt to swim.

At the weekends they were invited to large mildewed houses in the country. They learnt by observation to eat peas from the back of a fork, and not to say 'no thank you' when they wanted a second helping; in Jerusalem it would be considered most impolite not to refuse a dish at least seven times before finally surrendering to the entreaties of your host.

In their third year they received a visit from the young Prince Farouk, then a cadet at Dartmouth Naval College. A makeshift party, with the usual selection of broken undergraduate china, was held in his honour at their digs in Queens'.

The prince was particularly interested in the question of how discipline was maintained during the weekend, and when it was explained that the proctor patrolled with two bulldogs who would escort revellers back to their respective colleges, he was naturally curious to know how these dogs could always distinguish between an undergraduate reveller and a townee.

After the three years the twins returned home in a third-hand Studebaker along the coast of North Africa. They spent their first night at the Hotel St Georges, above the verandahs a façade of mauve and white bougainvillaeas; in the morning weaving through the ginnels of the kasbah, the thick local dialects of the traders as if their ears were full of water.

In Tunis they bought Berber rugs for Mama and Anastasia, discounted cigars for Anton and Baba. They were mistaken for Englishmen by the guide. As the shabb told the shopkeeper he would return later for his commission, the twins casually enquiring – and what figure do you usually receive?

'Ya Allah. Ya Allah. You are my brothers. May God forgive me.' The guide refusing his fee, the twins having to pin his arms against the wall and force the coins into his pockets.

Petrol was scarce, they used up all their spare cans; they would divert to army camps to bargain for more fuel. Before leaving Cambridge they had instructed their tailor to sew secret pouches invulnerable to pickpockets into the linings of their jackets; when they extricated their cash they twisted and writhed as if they had fleas.

Due to the unseasonal rains all the bridges over the flooded rivers were down; the twins paid the village children who ran after the car to wade ahead to gauge the depth of the waters and the firmness of the bed.

In the coffee houses of Benghazi they were told that the road to Egypt was lost under landfalls and sand winds, a deliberate policy to impede passage between the countries in the event of war. They followed the web of tracks east through the dunes; the charts from the Automobile Association in Leicester Square innacurate and misleading, every evening they worked on correcting and re-mapping the itinerary.

At the Egyptian border, sleeping in the house of a Greek who took in travellers, supping on succulent gazelle; the broken windows stuffed with rags to prevent the freezing air blowing the sand in; the following morning they asked their host if that remote spot had a name, and he told them it was called El-Alamein: the two signposts.

Above the bay at Alexandria, they stripped, and wandered through the beach cabanas among the fallen columns in the clear waters.

The glistening oil road to Cairo poured over the sands by the Shell Oil Company, on the horizon the growing tips of the pyramids like the jaws of a sunken land-trap.

After two nights at Shepheard's Hotel, buying more cigars for Baba and Anton, chocolates and petits fours for Mama and Anastasia at Groppi Patisserie, driving through the irrigated sahloon towards Sinai, over the canal, a roll of thunder like the beating of the drums before dawn during Ramadan, great dark storm clouds gathering over the desert.

Following camel-tracks between rusted petrol cans and rolling tumbleweed, the car losing its grip in the mud-slides, through the mists a shabb leading a mule loaded with charcoal for his village; with his assistance fitting the triple-chains on to the tyres, the man tucking the baksheesh of Groppi chocolates under his abaya for his daughter.

The way continuing wet and treacherous; on the high dunes the doors open so they could jump clear as the car slipped.

That evening they reached an isolated police post by the name of Bir-Hasana, the guards offering shelter in the corrugated-iron barakiyeh, a share of their rations of boiled eggs, stale bread and water; the twins opening the tins and ribboned boxes from Groppi.

By night the reflection of the moon on the damp sand providing sufficient light to read by.

Each morning they pleaded to be allowed to continue, every day contriving a more dramatic excuse – a cousin's christening, a sister's wedding, their father's funeral.

On the fourth day the two brothers pacing in a circle around the hut, kicking at the drying sand. From the shade of the sahra canopy the senior officer watching, laughing. 'The Jews wandered forty years in this desert, and you have been here only four days . . .'

In the late afternoon the twins reaching the border town of Beersheba to be told they must not continue their journey by night; snipers were shooting from the cover of the hills along the Hebron Road; over the preceding months Arab militias had attacked railways, bridges, telephone lines, main roads leading to the new Jewish settlements.

A garrulous Sudanese guard riding between the dark ridges.

'Fear not for only Fate decrees the moment of death.

'A man is warned in a prophetic dream that his son will die before he reaches manhood; on waking the father becomes alarmed, and locks the boy in a room, refusing him any visitors lest he come to harm, but one day a friend takes pity on the son, and brings him a water-melon as a gift; the father takes the melon to the room, the boy cuts a first slice: the snake coiled within the fruit rears up its head and bites the boy.

'What is written is written.'

On the exposed stretches, the twins ducking under the dashboard.

A full moon that night, the car an easy target, but the snipers preferring to stay in on clear nights for fear of being seen themselves.

They arrive to find the streets of Jerusalem deserted, the curfew in force since dusk, at the roadblocks the dust-caked Studebaker with its GB plates ushered on towards the silent newly lit avenues of Mamilla.

On the first day the road to the coast was clear, the twins driving down through the untilled hills of barwaq and prickly pear to visit Anton in Jaffa.

With them they took the young niece of Herr Walter; for months she had been waiting for her parents to arrive from Munich; like her aunt, Ariane had clear cornflower eyes, hair bright as ripe lemons, her jawline and cheek-bones sharp as a gemstone you could cut your fingers on.

Beyond the plains of orange groves, down between the new tenements of Tel Aviv, the white paint already flaking in the strong sunlight, a reek of tanning and boiled cabbage; along the old mole the outlines of the cranes a giant score against the open sky.

The customs house in the sandstone serail above the port, a constant clattering from the sit-up-and-beg Underwoods, a cool winding passage through to the silence of the inner office, on the ceiling a large fan slowly turning, over the windows the slatted blinds down against the glare from the waters.

In the half-light the brothers kiss, exchange gifts; all the delicacies from Groppi have been eaten in the desert, but the twins have saved Anton two boxes of Perfectos.

Ariane standing on the ledge, prying open the blinds, peering down the long quay. The passengers so thin and pale, like clothes drawn in along a washing-line, fur stoles, bombergs, astrakhan coats, patent pumps catching the noon sun, through the fierce light the figures stumbling on their sea legs, the steerage passengers pulling off their shirts, their chests narrow and sheeny as basted chickens, hamals picking the cases on to trollies, but their hands still groping the empty air as if at invisible bars.

That night Pascal drives Ariane back alone to the one-room apartment she shares with Herr Walter and Geli in Tel-Pioth on the western outskirts of the city, and as the still unwashed Studebaker is lost between the wide shadows of the eucalyptus trees under the avenue so my father also disappears from his own story; his will be the voice of a recording angel, the fact of his testimony the only evidence that unlike the others he would never forsake his brother.

Later that year Pascal bought a photographic supplier's and small studio beside the Allenby Hotel on the Jaffa Road. Over the door the polished tin signs exotic as hieroglyphs; Agfa, Carl Zeiss Jena, Leica, Ilford.

An umber light through the dusty windows, over the cool stone floor a long oak secretaire, in rosewood cabinets behind green-tinted glass, the lenses, films, leather-bound albums, as if sunk deep underwater; in the thin drawers of the tallboy, the photographic papers: velour, semi-matt, sepia, gloss.

He kept on the existing staff. Tsvi, the retired Yiddish watchmaker who repaired the broken cameras; the Armenian orphan Chant with his withered leg, a survivor of the death marches across the deserts of Northern Iraq, his elders still calling him 'boy' though he was already in his late forties.

In the dark room, his maternal uncles Krikor and Livon, and paternal uncle Hagob. The old men can no longer see in the daylight, and every evening Chant guides his uncles between the carossas and fruit lorries to the shuttered hostel rooms Pascal has rented on the lower end of the Allenby Road.

Each morning as the customers return he slips the pictures into the leather presentation wallets, his fingers tracing the gold indentations of the emblem, a camel with his driver at the old city gates, this motif never failing to delight him though he passes the scene it describes every day without pausing to notice it.

With so many tourists business is brisk, all afternoon Pascal sits in the Bristol Café over the road with the professional photographers working on albums of the Holy Land in photogravure, at noon Chant limping up past the post office with the takings of the morning to the new Barclays Bank.

In the small studio over the back courtyard, the rack of canvas flaps and backgrounds for the old-fashioned portraits: the façade of a rococo palace, a willow-sheltered pond under a silver moon, a balustrade before a distant prospect of snow-turbaned mountains. His favourite he took to decorate the inner wall of his apartment upstairs; over the white sands of a deserted bay, a white villa below hills of umbrella pines.

Later when the family had disowned him he would meet Ariane in that room, the blinds closed to the street, the velvet divan shuddering from the heavy fruit lorries below, both peering up at the view of the villa on the island as if from a bobbing pleasure launch.

In the first year of the war he would still drive Ariane down to the port at Jaffa, this journey now a regular day-trip, the quay empty of immigrants, the docked ships loaded with grain and arms for the British garrisons.

In the waterside cafés, the farmers who had grown rich selling the surrounding bayyaras to the settlers showing off their Jewish mistresses; they would stand out of the wind at the stalls selling fresh orange sorbet and iced halves of water-melon, the lapis-blue of the calm sea the rim of that great bowl the future was raising to her lips.

When they had not argued she would lie with her head on his lap, her nails pressed into the palm of his hand. From the stone parapet they look down over the weed-slicked rocks, the blood-orange sun sinking into the dark waters; the dock lights coming up, their brightness dimming the stars.

On the way back they would stop in Lydda, at the house of his cousin Boulos, the priest. A great bear of a man with a twin-pointed beard like an Old Testament prophet, he sits on the verandah puffing on his narghile, nodding to his parishioners, his slight Syrian wife Samia bringing through fuul-medames and baba-ganoush, Ariane dipping in with her dirty fingers, scraping the plate with a warmed ghif, only asking later what it was she had eaten.

With so many distinguished musicians among the immigrants, Herr Walter had less work as a music teacher, as did Geli, and so because she had talent when she was old enough Ariane had begun to play piano with the Mandelbaum Orchestra at the King David Hotel. Each afternoon Anastasia would take tea on the terrace with her bridge circle, in their long white robes with scarlet sashes the suffragi weaving between the rattan loungers and the billowing silk dresses of the officers' wives; the manager Arnie Hamburger arranging the tables so her brother would have a clear view of the band.

After the thé-dansant he would meet Ariane in one of the vacant suites on the top floor. She would lie naked looking out of the window, her hunched shoulder-blades like the stumps of lost wings, through the partly drawn curtains the view of the golden dome above the grey walls, flat as the canvas drops in the old studio.

In that first year of the war he never touched her, not even to kiss her cheek, or hold her hand. Always he would give her the negatives and prints, the leather wallets with the emblem of the camel-driver at the gates sold to buy bully-beef and gherkins for her Uncle Walter; on her solitary walk back to Tel-Pioth, the torn fragments gusting down the wadis on the night winds.

Sometimes they ate together, but she would not let him be seen walking her home. The dining-room in the hotel, a Pharaoh's barge, blue lilies and lotus flowers curling over the gilded pilasters and roof-joists, Camembert smuggled across the lines from Beirut, camel meat passing as beef under the cover of the chef's rich sauces.

Ariane gazing across to the other tables as if at a cinema screen; the jewellery of the Syrian and Egyptian princesses flickering like desert fires across the candlit shadows.

But one night they were spied together by the cousin of the maid Jamila who worked in the pantries.

For weeks afterwards when he walked up from the Jaffa Road through the newly asphalted avenues of Mamilla to the old house she would tell him that Anastasia and Mama were not at home, and close the door. As always Baba would be sitting out in the shade of the narghile verandah; for many years he had been deaf, and when Pascal knelt to kiss his hand, he stroked his hair as if he was still a boy, and over his forehead he made the sign of the cross.

His telephone calls to Anton in Jaffa were never answered.

On the day the Arabs rioted in the old city, his supplies from England had still not been cleared from the quay. He drove down through the curfew-deserted roads to the sandstone serail above the port. In the outer rooms the secretaries behind the Underwoods told him Anton had not come to the office that morning; along the cool winding passage, hanging wraiths of cigar smoke.

From the window he watched the quay burn, over the

crates of developing chemicals, a gloriole of livid purple and gold; the virgin's crown.

He returned to find the windows of the shop had been shattered, the tin signs twisted in the gutter, the silver anaglyphs under the broken emblem of the camel-driver strewn over the street, smeared with mud, donkey faeces.

From that day on he would keep the shutters halfway down; within business continuing as usual.

When he sat at teatime on the terrace the following week, a raven-haired girl had taken Ariane's place at the piano. Anastasia was not at her usual table; in the lobby Arnie Hamburger explaining that his sister and her bridge circle would not return until Ariane had been removed from the band.

As he walked out along the hillside, the ground rose up under his feet, and he was thrown face-down into the road. He looked back, the entire east wing of the hotel had collapsed like a house of cards.

For three nights he would listen to the cries of those trapped under the rubble grow gradually weaker, and on the fourth night he could not sleep for the silence.

With the profits from the photographic supplier's, Pascal bought a strip of uncultivated land in the hills to the west of the city. There he built a precise replica of the white villa on the canvas drop.

Broad marble steps under a colonnade to the portico, cast-iron grilles under the windows, vine trellises over the verandahs, low-slanting roofs of rose slates quarried in the deserts of Petra.

In the level below the lawns he concealed the first private swimming-pool in the city, the surround of tessellated tiles imported from Tuscany; he had never learnt to swim.

The house encircled with high walls, thin crests of cream over the cobalt-painted bricks, the fallow borders covered with dunes of sand, an illusion of softly lapping waves, but from the upper floor through the olive terraces still the view of old Jerusalem crowned with its golden dome.

Pascal refused to leave the villa. The local patisseries would not serve Ariane; the maid brought up provisions from the city.

On the evening of the epitafio, he watched the distant processions of flickering homeward candles between the dark hills, and sat up all the night boiling the eggs trussed with strings dipped in beet dyes. In the morning they drank arak, and played the pecking-game until only one patterned egg remained unbroken; in the nest of silk scarves under her dressing-table, she conceals the victor, as if waiting for it to hatch.

On days there was no sniping and the curfew had been lifted, Walter and Geli would walk up through the terraces, and stay late into the evening. All afternoon Pascal would prepare in the kitchen.

The filo pastry he cast like a net over the olive-wood table until it was thin and transparent as muslin; the baclava crisp and fagile as long-dead eucalyptus leaves.

The cod's roe and stale bread soaked in hot water, churned with olive-oil, lemon and milk, until it was the faint pink of her flush.

He took parsley and mint from the troughs on the verandah, the widest leaves from the vine, with the thick veins on the inside rolling together the tomatoes, onions, black peppers and rice, the dolmades laid to cook slowly on a bed of chard and parsley stalks.

In the font under the vines, the bottles of claret Walter and Geli had brought from Richon-le-Zion.

When she drinks she remembers autumn walks in the English Gardens, wading through fallen leaves, her mother telling her to keep to the open spaces.

She looks down from the littered bower of the Chinese

Tower past the Kunsthalle to the black roofs of their apartment building on Prinzregentenplatz, on the edge of the woods by the lake where she is forbidden to play, men in braces and lederhosen stumbling from the beer-trestles, mouthing words she has never heard, falling under the leaves, and like the stucken she casts in the pond they do not rise up again.

By nightfall as the fellahin bring in their asses through the orange orchards, the music drifting over the high walls.

They play along to the HMV gramophone, the lid-speaker propped on the window-ledge, the restless travelling of the concertos a consolation for their own confinement: Bach's 1st; Vivaldi in A Minor, no 61.

The momentum of a carriage hurtling away from a pursuer only to draw ever more inescapably towards him, the highways of notes swaying between caution and conviction, calculation and compulsion, elegy and anticipation, between repose and frenzy, a deft exhilaration predicated upon pure dread.

For light relief, the andantes of Mozart's concertos, the mock pathos of Suzanna and Barbarina's lament for the lost pin, perfect harmonies without finality, without tragedy, like Narcissus delightfully imprisoned by the immaculate reflection of their own virtuosity.

Ariane playing the solo parts, careless in the swell of the recorded tutti, an ever widening river as it nears final dissolution, her plaintive cantilena seeking consolation in its own transient beauty, her lonely notes carried over in an ominous parody by the scratching tutti like captives apparelled for a triumph.

When the wine is finished the patterns of the ritornello relentlessly returning upon themselves, miming the stepped symmetries of half-forgotten dances; the later adagio holding up the melancholy of its lost pleasures like an empty cup.

By the first week of May the settler militias had fought their way to the untilled telat above the quarter, between the rocks and wild figs the barrels of the Enfields stolen from the British depot glinting in the cold spring sunlight. The wealthier families began to take unseasonal holidays.

'It will all blow over in a couple of days.' That English refrain suddenly fashionable once more, as if the fighting were just a spell of inclement weather.

Those who left entrusting their keys to the families who had stayed, their children climbing into the empty gardens, festooning themselves with the clothes on the washing-lines, stripping the orchards of plums and acadiniah.

Anton had fled the bombardment of Jaffa, and returned home. But in the second week the gunmen came down from the heights, and told those remaining to leave their houses with what they could carry, the long slow file of families escorted by the blue-eyed youths under the city walls into the ornate façade of the YMCA, as if to a waiting cruise-liner.

Baba was too frail to walk, and Anton and Elias the gardener carried him over their shoulders in his full black robes. Mama and Anastasia brought only single small suitcases; they would not allow themselves to be seen by the neighbours bearing any greater load.

The column from Mamilla were corralled in the lower offices and locker-rooms. Each row was shared by three families, the high-jump palliasses given over as beds to the elderly and the women, sheets hung between the wall-pegs for privacy; they took turns showering and washing their clothes behind curtains improvised from spare dresses and towels.

The men were not allowed to leave the building, but each morning Mama and Anastasia would walk back through the deserted avenues to the house. On the first day they brought out the three oldest icons, on the second silver salvers wrapped in guilloche shawls.

On the third day a fair-haired youth was waiting at the head of the drive. Mama was carrying the rocaille mirror, when she could not understand his foreign words, he pushed against the glass with the butt of his rifle. Over the unwatered soil of the cyclamen bed, the broken shards, she glances down to see a dozen cloudless skies.

From that day Mama would never look again at her own reflection; her hair uncombed, growing rank as her untended gardens; through his failing eyes Baba sees again the wild girl he first loved.

When he heard what had happened for the first time in two years Pascal left the house, and ran with Ariane to the YMCA. He was told the family had already fled, in a hired car, a navy-blue Chevrolet; for the Lebanon border.

In the villages beyond the city he found only empty streets, in the alleys and squares carcasses of dogs and donkeys black with flies, a sign to the families who had dared remain.

By midday he had reached Lydda. The road through the outskirts blocked by the sahra and palm-frond shelters of those who had fled the fighting in the cities on the coast.

At the corner of the main square, the vines and reed shades stripped from the front verandah of the house of Boulos and Samia. Out on the bare stoop, Chant with his three old uncles, all sweating in their heavy coats, standing in line beside their cardboard suitcases as if waiting at a platform, from their canvas bags a stench of rancid meat, flies settling over their mauve-stained wrists and hands.

Under the trailing trellis, the door ajar, he ushers them into the cool interior, but they will not enter. He calls into the empty rooms, no one answers.

On the night march from Jerusalem blind Hagob and Livon had been told the soldiers had used the wife of the priest roughly, and returning from the café he had battered her with the base of a narghile to save his own honour, the neighbours dragging her unconscious body to the sanctuary of the mosque; on the beam in the yard he had hung himself, the wood had broken under his weight, and he had stumbled out into the fields towards the positions of the enemy.

From the window he watches the square. Under the boarded façades of the shops, scattered glass, upturned chairs, strands of raffia and cotton spinning over the sand in the warm breeze through the valley. For weeks the grocers and traders of the quarter had waited for the promised Bedouin of Mitghal Pasha, but when the tribesmen came they had looted and raped before riding on southwards into the plains above Ramleh.

From the radios in the alleys behind the house the wail of the nationalist songs like the keening of children in the night; Falastin with its loping rhythms, its camel's gait.

Along the edges of the square tall tanaki of gasoline and grain requisitioned from the Jerusalem train to barter for the weapons promised by King Abdulla to defend the town, the exposed surfaces of the mounds of flour a shivering sheet of flies and weevils, over the sandblown pavements the town militia swaggering out to scatter those from the shelters feeding on the lower flanks damp from the seeping petrol.

One shabb bragging that his gun has a range of twenty miles, a rice merchant that his bullets could pierce the breasts of three men, over their shoulders a motley collection of tommy-guns, Stens, Berber and Ottoman hunting rifles; the unbroken windows on the upper storeys reflecting the high sun, the square a hall of mirrors.

When the refugees have dispersed the town militiamen stare up into the cloudless sky, still waiting for Abdulla's aeroplanes, others on the rooftops watching for the dust clouds of the promised arms lorries, but by noon the only arrivals in the square are a band of travelling entertainers, dancers, musicians, painted singers; on a fruit cart an ancient gramophone blaring Umm Kulthoum's Ghanni li Shwei up the deserted alleys; in disgust the guards fire rounds among the hooves of their asses, and the players take flight; later there was word they had been ambushed and stripped by the Bedouin down on the plain.

It is the last Saturday of Ramadan, in the heat of the afternoon the militiamen invisible in the gutted hollows of the abandoned shops, across the pavements lone figures staggering faint from the fasting; above on the ledges of the flat roofs, crows gathering.

At dusk the hum of aeroplane engines high in the darkening sky, a slow shower of white leaflets like pantomime snow. Under the fallen trellis Chant lights a match, on the mimeographed sheet, a crude cartoon: Abdulla and Farouk and the Mufti in a leaking tug-boat sinking under stylised waves; he remembers the early rhetoric of the Arab nationalists, 'And we will drive the sons of the dead mother into the sea.'

After the call of the muezzin at nightfall, the radios behind the house all playing Falastin, the sirens sounding in the outskirts, at Dinyan, Innabeh, at Al-Kiyat; schoolboys and shuyyuk clutching axes, shovels and clubs, running out of the lanes after the guards, but all prove false alarms.

As the first shells fall to the south along the Ramleh Road, Chant tells the old men it is only the tambours of the travelling players, and Livon and Krikor stuff their ears with cotton balls, and lie under their coats on the warm tiles; those guards with English rifles leaving the cover of the shops to find the Arab troops encamped at Beit Nubada, but after three hours they have not returned.

In the square by the pump barakiyeh, the radio-operator trying to contact the Jordanians, but all they hear is Radio

Jerusalem, Beethoven's 2nd playing to a background tim-
pani of small-arms fire and mortar crumps like hollow
clapping.

The guards have three antiquated artillery pieces abandoned by the British, but no meters, and few shells. They
fire into the darkness, their range falling short, to the east
the petrol supplies in the water-tower burning across the
sky as if dawn had risen at midnight.

The sand winds driving the flames back into the outskirts
of the town, Chant and Pascal remembering the wartime
bombing drills in preparation for the Italian raids which
had never come, sheltering together in the fireplace.

At dawn they cannot see their reflections in the window for the soot; for the first time in a thousand years
the muezzin has not been called from the tower of the
mosque, everyone still sleeping, the Haganah soldiers walking through the deserted trenches and barricades without
firing a single shot.

The few surprised guards scurrying back from their
overrun positions to hide their weapons were cornered in
the alleys, and rounded up in the lower square. From the
house they heard the distant burst of a grenade like a carpet
being beaten over a balcony, the old woman's cackling of
the tommy-guns.

From the silence of the Sunday streets loudspeakers
calling all men to the grand mosque, old Hagob struggling
down from the verandah, Krikor and Livon calling him
back, stumbling out into the square; unsighted by the
bright morning light, they trip on the sandblown pavements,
clutching blindly at the broken shop-fronts; Chant pulling
them back behind the door.

Still covered in soot, Pascal wipes small slits in the dust
over the windows of the Studebaker; he can see out, but is
invisible within. He drives alone towards the mosque, in the
lower square the piled bodies under the white lime-powder

like a new municipal monument waiting to be assembled, along the roadside soldiers ordering the men of larger stature out of the line towards the fields; he recognises a fat café-singer, a barber, two novice priests who had called at the house when he had sat on the verandah with Ariane hungry after their long drive through the hills. From the acadiniah orchards beyond the fields, the hacking cough of the machine-guns.

He pulls the Studebaker into a small yard, noses under a pile of woodchips until the car is completely covered. When he wakes it is morning again, the mosque surrounded by soldiers, a stench of urine and faeces, from within a continual crying out for water; three gun-boys urinating in the ablution trough, and though it was daylight during Ramadan there were those who lowered their heads like cattle and drank.

Along the road those vehicles whose batteries had been removed by their owners being dragged by mules towards the square.

His the only car following the march southwards out of the town. Among the crowd he saw the maid Jamila who had closed the door of his own house to him in those weeks after he had first been spied at the hotel with Ariane; as he draws towards her, the women dropping through the camel-thorn into the ditch.

Further on he passes men winding money-belts around the waists of their wives and mothers, hiding gold piastres in socks, their watches in the pockets of children, fountain pens and ear-rings among swaddling clothes.

The column led southeastwards, from the main road, over the sahool; on the roof of an abandoned carossa a wild-eyed youth with a loud-hailer calling down, 'You are all going to King Abdulla who sold you each for half a piastre.' The road tapering into a track between hills and ravines, the way overgrown with gorse and prickly pears, on the ridges the black outlines of the soldiers against the brilliant sun. When the column slowed they shot into the air. Behind the hills, the hovering engines of unseen aeroplanes like hives of troubled bees.

At the end of the track the march narrowing to a single file through a cluster of irregulars, he drives the car up along the side of the low tel; at the feet of the gunmen, glass jars filled with bracelets and watches, an intense shimmering of silver and gold as if at the front stall in the jewellery soukh.

Those wearing clean suits were being dragged into the hollow, their wrists checked for strap marks, their shoes removed to search for coins; their feet catching on the sharp stones, a trail of dried blood across the white earth to the cover of the wadis.

By noon the earlier march had reached the level sahel east of the village of Jimzu. The water-skins empty, the sun high and hot, the elderly staggering like drunkards. He would never forget the howling of the women and children.

The younger members of the families taking turns with the suitcases, alongside the path, discarded jugs, bags, clothes. He heard rumours of routes to hidden wells, but most proving false trails.

As it was summer the wells were dry, the drawing-ropes broken, and men tied shirts together, and were lowered into the mud to suck out the water; one shabb was pushed into the hole, and the crowd fell on him, and licked him naked. In the jostling and fighting around the base of the wells many lost their shoes, and had to be carried on the shoulders of their brothers.

Some chewed on cornstalks and sugar-cane, others queued to pay a fellah for the use of his ewe; he saw mothers with babies crouched behind bushes yielding their breasts to the faltering.

In the shade of wild figs, young men lying alone, waiting for the old fathers and grandfathers they had lost at the wells, other shebab had wrenched the money-belts from their elders and hurried on ahead, many of the shuyyuk did not surrender their belts and were whipped on like beasts by the young men.

On the parched plain before Ni'ilin he came upon the remnants of the previous march, twitchings under humped blankets, in the sunken gulleys the crying of abandoned children, down on the banks babies suckling on their dead mothers, on the crossing paths dazed women clutching dead children to their breasts; those who had drunk wine were kissing the bodies of the fallen, sucking the moisture from their tongues and gums, and under a leafless tree the old Sheikh-of-the-telephone calling above their bowed heads over the barren plains.

And when the blast shall sound
Upon the day when a man shall flee from his brother,
His mother, his father,
Then shall all faces be covered in dust
And the sky in darkness.

At the foot of the tree, he opened the door of the car, and the Sheikh did not recognise him, but out of charity spat into his face.

He followed the trail of discarded grain sacks, rugs, silver pots, bowls, before nightfall reaching the shade of the olive groves outside Ni'ilin; a younger Sheikh wandering among the prone bodies, mutttering prayers, the villagers waiting in the zucchini field until the refugees threw down gold piastres; the mukhtar bringing up bread, sardines, hard-boiled eggs and water.

Those going back with food and jugs of water to elderly relatives were pulled under by the oncoming crowd, many did not return. Some hid their jugs under their abayas; on the wastes they met old neighbours pleading for water for their mothers and aunts who drank with modesty only for shebab to fall upon the jar which would be broken.

Mothers who had entrusted their children to those with mules and carts returned to find the animals shot, their raw flesh eaten away, and on the darkening banks of the dried wells they could no longer see the faces of the shaking bodies.

But the young who had gone back out of pity were rewarded for when they returned to the olive groves below Ni'ilin they found only charred limbs among the smoking stumps of the trees. Above invisible in the night sky, the circling drone of the aeroplanes.

In Ramallah the incoming roads as if on the day of the bazaar, at every corner the refugees bartering watches and rings for bread and beans, shebab clambering on the roof, on the doors and bonnet; he had to brake abruptly to shake them off so he could see through the slit in the dust.

On a balcony above the teeming square, a slight lady in a waisted silk kaftan scattering sugared almonds and nougat, laughing as the mob fought, and throwing down more.

The next morning he took the coast road towards the border. If not for the silence it might have been market day, the fellahin leading donkeys laden with grain, chickens in boxes, their eyes lowered, the old women with straw panniers on their heads stuffed with fruit and bedding; the soldiers keeping their distance among the burnt-out sahra huts.

Beyond Acre the new asphalt road built by the British blocked by boulders and barbed-wire. Down on the shingle where the ground was firm he followed the line of cars, their roofs piled high with trunks and cages; he passed vehicles half-submerged in the tide, others stranded on the damp sands like dying whales; the seats and linings being stripped by the bands of Bedouin waiting behind the dunes.

Years before the new road had been built, wire-netting had been laid where the course was most treacherous, rusted tangles ripping the tyres of the leading cars, families wading on through the wash with what they could carry.

In the early evening the grooves in the sands led up the beach towards the flickering lights of the border village of Naquoura. Beyond the black slick of cracked asphalt, roadblocks set up by the Arab and Jewish irregulars, columns of refugees herded through a narrow isthmus between two hillocks; the nearer composed of surrendered rifles, the further of confiscated grain sacks, panniers, suitcases; over the mounds drifting smoke from the fires burning the carcasses of the mules and asses.

He drives along the bed of a dark wadi to the outcrop above the checkpoint, the crest guarded by a single Haganah youth. As he edges the car forward, the boy raises his rifle. He winds down the window, his words across the clearing in a Hebrew so pure it was as if an ancient prophet had called out from the wilderness, but the youth spoke only Yiddish, and taking Pascal for a deranged rabbi he lifted his rifle and broke both the headlamps of the Studebaker.

He could see nothing; the lights of the village hidden by the headland; across the border the hard-edged hills of Jabal Amil no more than creases in the humid curtain of the night.

He returned to find makeshift shelters of waterproof sheeting and corrugated iron along the outer walls of the house.

It was a cold winter for those from the coast. Many had never seen the mountains and the snow.

When he heard there was cholera among the barakiyat he locked the gates, and would no longer allow the maid to take food out among the refugees.

At dawn he woke to the cracking of ice broken by rocks, the chants of the women coming up from the well under the terraces; over the walls, the earthenware pitchers bobbing slowly upwards; Ariane remembering the lobster pots they had watched from the quay being drawn in on the tide.

In Beirut, Anastasia and Anton shared a two-room flat with Baba and Mama, one block back from the corniche.

Baba was too frail to manage the stairs, but Anton would bring him Turkish coffee and cigarettes from the stands on the Raoche. There was no electricity; in the heat, the ice-box flooding the loosely tiled floors.

Baba refuses to eat, he takes only spoonfuls of tea. He lies with his arms in a cross over his body; he tells Anastasia and Mama not to move his arms when he sleeps.

At the funeral the cathedral and the courtyard outside crowded with mourners, many his old parishioners whom he had baptised and married, now also refugees in Beirut.

The pale exiles passing the open coffin like ghosts at their own funeral, the old order of the Ottoman gentry born into a timeless world which had disappeared into their memories like a great ship going down under the waters.

When three months later Mama died, the priests would not allow her body to be laid in the ecclesiastical graveyard adjoining the cathedral. Her coffin was taken on a cart to the Greek Orthodox cemetery at Ashrafieh in the hills east of the city.

Anton and Anastasia did not have enough money to pay the fares to keep up the grave. After the civil war began, they could no longer cross to the eastern sector.

For months on end Pascal never leaves the house. He has become a stranger in his own land. He forgets himself in music, in Ariane; like tender scar-tissue, the gentle ripening of her body over that loss he can never repeal.

Jerusalem, a divided city; severed from the quarters of his

95

youth as if from his own arms and legs, from St Georges, from St Stephen's Gate; his childhood already remote as the picturesque scenes in the prints of old Palestine by Roberts hung along the corridors of the villa.

In the still wells of her eyes he sees the past she had never known. Under the walls, the queue of taxi-carossas, in the shade the shoeblacks with their polished stools, the bustling cafés filled with the cameleers and market-traders; the air heavy with the smoke of bubbling narghiles and the steaming manure of the cattle and donkeys piled high with wheat and melons from the plains.

Wherever he walks he has the sense he is being followed; by the Shin Beth; by ghuls. As if by the legerdemain of an illusionist, the city reconfigured around him until he can no longer trust his own memories; the alleys of tailors, shirt-makers, butchers, all half-empty, in the dark hollows untended ranks of sullen plate-souvenirs; the café opposite his shop, a kosher restaurant.

The larger Mamilla houses now occupied by several families, the gardens divided with chicken-wire, planted over with potatoes, cabbages, zucchini.

The family house bulldozed to make way for a new hotel, its balconies opening to the same views over the walled city; only the ruined windmill surviving, strung with wire pots of geraniums, the picturesque centrepiece of a roundabout.

Some weekends, for old time's sake, they go out to the Pharaoh's dining-room at the King David Hotel; coffee and mints afterwards on the uncomfortable Morris chairs in the lounge; Japanese and Yemeni Jews thronging the lobby like extras from a neighbouring set.

Through a crowd in the bridge hall he glimpses Harpo Marx; he remembers the antic spectre in the tin-hut cinema, goes forward to shake his hand, the broad-chested body-guards of the prime minister closing ranks, and with the tired indulgence of sanatorium nurses guiding him gently towards the sliding doors.

In other cities the past yielding willingly or under duress to its own renewal, but here only a sudden eviction, the new tenants with the innocence of children making up their den from what others have discarded.

In those first cold winters they travelled via Cyprus to Cairo.

On the windswept terrace at Shepheard's he remembers the story the barman had told ten years before. 'A fashionable lady wishes to be seen talking with the legendary Lawrence; she approaches with the remark, "Eighty-four today, Colonel." He replies, "And many happy returns."'

Always the thin edge of guilt in her laughter, like silk tearing.

In the shuttered bar of the Gezirah Sporting Club, only wizened lounge-lizards, women of dubious reputation; beyond the deserted lido and polo field, they stroll among the dusty headstones of the pet cemetery.

Along the brown river, the houseboats lilting in the mud, half-sunk charred hulls, the lights of the remaining bordellos like lost necklaces in the shoreline scum.

Under the ruined pergolas of Groppi Patisserie, a fly-blown corner shop, the glass encrusted with the sand of the khamsin; he tells her the wind of fifty days commemorates the time when Cain carried the body of his brother through the desert in search of a burial-place.

They take a taxi on New Year's Eve to a party at the Mena House Hotel by the pyramids. Among his retinue of gamblers and full-bodied whores, the tallow-pale monarch with his four chins flicking grapes at the bare backs of the dancing ladies.

As they leave, the head waiter following on to the lit-up drive. 'Sir, His Highness has a message; here the

97

dogs have not learnt to distinguish the students from the townees.'

Alongside the avenues into the city the moonlight on the wings of the moths; in the shadows, the eyes of beggars.

1985–1989

I

But when you heard these stories, your head lowered in polite deference as at the reading of a scripture lesson, your eyes dim with hidden prospects, and if you spoke of your own family it was as though their history was as remote from your trances as those fragments of the past we had glimpsed through the rising condominiums, the ruined watchtowers below the carretera, the coves where the wreckers had waited with their false lights, and on the tobacco-smugglers' trails through the cork forests high above the resorts those forgotten tavernas to which only he could have shown you the way.

In London I studied for a postgraduate degree at the Warburg Institute, my mornings in the intimate gloom of the slide-theatre, the lecturer's pointer sweeping through tempera skies to scratch at peeling statues and colonnades, a bird timid of landing, my afternoons among the narrow stacks and periodical shelves of the basement-holdings; the catacomb murmurings of the researchers and the patter of the flat-soled shoes of the Courtauld girls along the parquet corridors slowly fading with the light until above only the slowing shuffle of old Gombrich like the final twitching of a wounded beast, high in the dark façade the lonely glow at his study window as I returned at dusk on the Metropolitan Line to the top-floor walk-up I had rented in North Kensington.

In the ashtrays, half-smoked cigarillos; on the window-ledges and the creased cushions, the smoothed chocolate-wrappings he used as bookmarks, the hardback volumes of Scott-Moncrieff, propped spine-up like models of Saxon long-halls; on the deal table, the plates of scrambled eggs he had not had time to finish.

I rarely saw my flat-mate, Crispian; he worked as the editor of a horse-breeding magazine on Lancaster Gate, returning late, leaving for the office before I had risen; since coming down to London he had lost touch with Reaper who had vacated the cottage in Yorkshire without paying his share of the rent and bills; the trail of forwarding numbers leading nowhere but back upon themselves, from Greenwich Village to Key West, from San Francisco to Greenwich Village.

In the evenings, I sit under the dormer window, and listen for his faltering words, and when she calls hear between her slurred insinuations distant music and the cicada-parsed silence of the hills, but most nights the telephone does not ring; the broken comb of low-rise estates against the sodium sky.

Her first and only visit had been brief. I had returned one afternoon to find her slumped on the stairs in the common parts, in ripped jeans and a long cashmere coat, her cracked cowboy-boots crossed over a single patent grip-bag, her eyes hooded and bloodshot from the journey, a porrito still smouldering on the runner's frayed edge.

She had told him she had come for her aunt's funeral, and it was only in the morning when I drove her down the Goldhawk Road to the Queen Charlotte Hospital that she had explained he was infertile and she had no money for the procedure, and throughout the day I had prepared the room with tiger-lilies and scented candles and a selection of videos for her convalescence, but when that evening I picked her up she had insisted I take her directly to Heathrow, and still woozy from the anaesthetic she had held her head out of the window and retched into the roadside; the stain like a broken wing that all the rains of that harsh winter would not wash away.

At first there were the letters, her scrawled blandishments like graffiti under his sullen crest, the post from the island slow and erratic, her fulsome pledges no more consolation than the light from a dying star; after two months the letters no longer came, and my own were not returned; in the darkened lecture-theatre the low voice telling of how Petrarch had asked a friend to write a letter purportedly from Homer so he might reply.

I had not forgotten the five-digit number on the Bakelite telephone in the panelled hall, after the long ringing her voice hushed and reverential, the holes in the mouthpiece filtering out every impurity, over the transoceanic silences her sighs and breathing as close as if I had held her sleeping head in my arms, but for weeks I would hear only the level tone of the engaged signal, and remember the curtained heat of the hotel rooms, the receiver clattering over the tiles as she found her rhythm, and on those few nights I came in late I would run to the answer-phone, a hunter returning to his trap, my ear to the black-plastic grid over the speaker as I played back the abrupt hang-ups and snatches of background hubbub; a detective who searches for crimes yet to be committed; through the window the breeze flicking between the open pages of my address book, the melancholy of those disused numbers like the dates of lost years.

And always the same dream, at first the scene where Grace Kelly is driving along the Riviera, the convertible spinning down the blind corners, through the umbrella pines a dazzling light, and from somewhere below the road a sound like a child stamping on a tin can, and afterwards all her cases forced, her clothes on the floor, his fine fingers playing the empty hangers like a xylophone and over the envelopes of my unopened letters in the inner pocket of the cashmere coat never cold enough to wear, and always the faltering voice of my father, and in the letters the perfect record of his words which every evening at the window I had failed to transcribe.

And so not wishing to sleep I would follow Shaman out into the night, each evening to a different club, on Mondays Limelight, on Tuesdays the Café de Paris, on Wednesdays Browns or the Wag, on Thursdays Crazy Larry's, but always the same desultory crowd, record-producers in black roll-necks and baggy turn-ups, gelled dealers grinding their teeth, pallid models in vinyl dresses like the wrapped white plums the campesinos brought down from the last grove, the crump of the hip-hop too loud to talk over yet everywhere the histrionic miming of a silent movie, and sometimes through the smoke and whirring lights I would spot one of the fops, and once I was certain I had glimpsed the caped Reaper, but by the time I had parted a way through the stomping bodies to the gallery I found only a mop-haired American college boy with a cartoon grin rubbing ice over his neck as he peered down at the shirtless break-dancer on the podium below.

In those years the clubs still closed early, and from the moment we had entered the velvet-curtained vestibule all the talk was already of private parties and after-hours venues, and during the evening people I did not know would greet me familiarly and tell me with an insinuating leer how we would meet later at the Ozbar, and by closing time I had always lost sight of Shaman, and those outside on the steps were trying to find the way to the Ozbar, and though some bragged of their last sessions there, no one ever seemed to remember the address, nor in what quarter of the city this establishment was situated.

One night I had gone with a tanned couple from the Wag

who claimed to know me from the island, to the Venus Flytrap on Old Compton Street, under a sex emporium of the same name, a side-entrance leading down into the dim unlicensed drinking-club, but that night we had found the iron door locked, on the pavement outside a pale young man in a foulard and velvet-collared crombie surrounded by a barracking circle of skinheads, above their chanting of 'PimpWhorePimp', his familiar plumm vocables floating out over the deserted alley.

'I wish you'd make up your minds, boys, then at least I'd know which way to dress.'

I walked alone to the taxi-rank, the man turning, calling after me, 'But, my dear, I'd remember that stitching anywhere.'

Gervase insisted on driving me home, and as I told him the name of my road he turned to me with a lewdly knowing look, and from an inner silk-lined pocket passed across a slim cut-glass phial which had once served as a button-hole vase, and out of politeness I took a perfunctory bump.

It was not until we had reached the first return that I realised we were not in the right building, the runner a darker ochre, a wide stripped door with a horse-head knocker where the stairs should have continued to the upper floor. He gave a short rap with the silver tip of his cane, and the door was opened by a bald homeboy with a broken nose, and we came up into a crowded hall, turbaned midget waiters weaving between dancers, thin drunk models swaying like reeds over the stream of prone bodies, and at the far end beside a brushwood fire dozing over an open book in the exact posture I still remembered from the low-lit bar of the Royal Hotel the unmistakable figure of Ozzy Rustum.

In the following months I no longer went to the nightclubs with Shaman, but once or twice a week would visit Rustum's after-hours salon in the neighbouring duplex;

that first long room like the store of a waxwork museum where characters from disparate places and epochs are lumbered with alien clothes and attitudes; only Gervase faithful to his original foppery; at the threshold like a temple beggar Palgrave always in the same patched corduroys and torn pullover laughing like a hyena at his own arcane jokes and bumming cigarettes from Foley who would surface from long sessions at his studio in Acton like some monster of the deep, his sleeves and collar dark with lime and terre-verte, a wrack of straw and bristle over his hair and shoulders, and through his after-trail of turpentine and porrito-smoke would emerge a crop-haired strawberry-blonde, the tailor's apprentice, the allegory of Fate with her eternal attributes of scissors and measuring-tape from the fitting-room overlooking the cathedral green whom Gervase had mischievously claimed was the daughter of a legendary rock star, and as a student at St Martin's she would always wear clothes of her own creation, baby-doll smocks trimmed with feather boas, rubber ball-gowns with mermaid-finned trails, and under the impression due to our public-school drawls and threadbare graces that she had penetrated the lowest circle of bohemian aristocracy she seemed almost offended not to be ignored.

It was there I had first encountered Anna again, and though Sylvie had told me her relationship with Reaper and her modelling career were over, still I had not expected to find her so changed, her untrained body so full and womanly, under an unkempt wiry bob her face bruised with pleasure's fatigues, and mistaking me for a dealer she had asked with a cracked lisp if I was holding the new love-pills, and I had pointed her towards the kitchen where the rough-house Dubliner Danny-boy presided over the Arabs and Persians with his pipes and silver-foil, but Anna had passed the door and stepped along the uncertain railing to the gravel-floored back-deck, and in her giddy high-heeled tottering against the first light of that winter dawn there remained no traces of her sister.

After a month with my father on the island I returned to the duplex to find Rustum and Foley and their intimates had withdrawn behind a locked door at the end of the windowless dog-leg passage where the bulbs had not been replaced, the hall given over to the Persians from the kitchen and the models and the slick-haired associates of Danny-boy, and sometimes Anna and Skye would stagger out with dishevelled clothes and wide eyes, gently caressing the rougher dealers as they tripped on to the terrace where they would clutch at each other in the frozen moonlight like flapper heroines under the shadow of the approaching beast.

The Persians ignored the girls, and kneeling under the wall-mounted telephone by the casement windows called the hooker agency before returning to their foil and pipes around the fire, and when half an hour later the Home-Counties belle in the leopard-lapelled two-piece was buzzed up by Danny-boy there seemed a faintly familiar tincture to her girlish blend of pugnacity and embarrassment, like the scent of a candy long out of production, and when she began wittily to mock the cod crests on their blazers the Persians forgot their imminent whore, and it was only afterwards as we drove to their mansion block in Marylebone that Gervase reminded me with the proprietorial pride in which an uncle might speak of a reformed miscreant niece that Punk Rose from the café had trained as an actress and would be making her debut the following month in a popular television series.

The apartment building was to the north of Marylebone High Road, the scrubbed red-brick lobby opening through a paved glassed-over atrium to an old-fashioned wooden-panelled escalator behind polished brass guard-rails, but they took the stairs, up through passages lined with glazed eau-de-Nil tiles to an embossed door with a hand-of-Fatima knocker.

The lounge like a waiting-room, on the coffee table ceramic ashtrays wedged among ancient copies of Time and National Geographic, along each wall a long scuffed leather sofa; in the skewed light of the upturned standard-lamp the Persians searching their pockets and the scraps of papers on the lilting shelves for the number of their contact for the love-pills, but each time they telephoned the line was engaged, and in the breaks before trying again they would squat like lost travellers over the blackened pleats of the foil.

Gervase surveying the scene with the vexed disdain of one who has found his way obstructed by public clowning, and they do not notice when we leave, the Wagner on the stereo so loud we do not speak as he drives through the silent streets of Paddington and Bayswater to a small square above Westbourne Grove, a church under scaffolding, over lustrous black railings a row of high white terraced houses.

He leans across, and raps with his cane on the window of the ground-floor flat, the curtain twitching, the door to the common parts opened by a stage Viking with straggling blond locks and anvil jawline, the mop-haired American from the upper gallery at Limelight; in the first room a cold glow from the halogen desk-lamps, the floor and walls in cream emulsion, dustsheets over the furniture, under the marble mantelpiece a small circular trampoline, and I wait looking over Gervase's shoulder as the boy pads barefoot into the bedroom; through the door on the wide secretaire a staffage of multi-vitamin containers and digital scales behind which Reaper is hunched like a medieval money-lender counting out the white pills into transparent change-sleeves.

The American leaning over the crowded surfaces, his

tentative fingers over Reaper's greying temple as if touching a rare pet through the gilded bars of its cage.

At first nothing happens. I sit on the floor, my back against the loose wainscoting. Through the locked door down the passage, the distant laughter of Palgrave, water running over glass.

On the bed Anna and Skye languorously stroking each other over the plump bolster; underneath Rustum lying pefectly still, the flaps of his tweed jacket like the shadows of wings.

A milky density to the half-light; a sense that I was not visible, my body abstracted into the entirety of the room; through the brocade curtains the rising sun like a dirty coin.

I am looking down upon myself. Anna nuzzling against my legs, shivering, as she pulls off her shirt she shakes her hair, a surfacing diver; at first rocking gently, her neck arched, easing my clenched fist inside her; her mouth snapping like a dolphin at its feed; a fearful shuddering, as if she were bearing a monster; and afterwards she clings to my sweat-damp neck, silently weeping.

That week Sylvie returned from the island. She had signed up for a three-month course at Parson's School of Fine Decoration on High Street Kensington, but flunked after the first week, claiming Monica was one of the principals; I later found this to be untrue.

She began to decorate the flat, but got no further than the bedroom door, scraping with loofahs, scumbling with sponges, daubing on grooved layers of varnish only to scratch away the hardened skin, and start again, and for the first time Crispian would come home early from the office, and repose with his Lindt and cheroots in the bath peering through the steam at her Penelope's labours as if she were some newly acquired sculpture he had not quite decided how to display.

But seeing her amidst so many coils and hanging twists I remembered only the snake we had passed on our last walk together into the hills, entangled in its old slough, its progress slackened by the drive of the wind, a prey for those normally its own quarry.

On the evenings we went to the Ozbar I was careful only I should pass her the love-pill, Skye and Gervase and Rose in the inner room lying close on the bed like a litter of kittens, but she would sit on her own in the corner, and run out slamming the door, and later I would find her in the kitchen with the Persians who had mistaken her for the girl they had called from the agency, and she was playing along, smirking vacantly, her shirt unbuttoned and loose off her arms, her tube-skirt riding up as she leant over the table to smoke from the foil, and as balding Amir rubbed his crotch between her buttocks she looked back at him with that same histrionic indifference of a wildebeest peering over its shoulders at the lion devouring its hindquarters, and for an hour outside the locked door I listened to her thin retching.

When Sylvie heard Anna had returned from the island, she would no longer go to the Ozbar; I would drive alone to the square off Westbourne Grove, the American boy with his cartoon grin unlocking both the doors, leading me through to the emulsioned sitting-room, in the bedroom a reverential silence, behind the wide desk Reaper concentrated among his canisters and scales like a scientist working late, raising his greying head as if from weighty lucubrations, and still I was not certain he had recognised me.

For days we would not leave the flat. We lived on Crispian's chocolates, and scrambled eggs. Our world shrank to the bed, and the windowless bathroom under the stairs, and yet when we had taken the pills we were masters of infinite space, alchemists of the four elements;

upstream she swims against the strong currents, a thrashing serpent given to the flames, soars and circles high above the scree; her thin rump in the air, she burrows the deeps, plucks out the earth's heart.

I would not know whether it was day or night, the alarm clock lost in the undergrowth of fallen books and unwashed clothes, across the bed the child's star of her splayed body, the grey twist of her anus, and I would pull the sheet up to her cold neck, and close the door tenderly as if I were still holding her sleeping head.

And though I left her with no key she would disappear for several days, and when she returned she would never speak of where she had been, and sometimes I found her slumped on the landing in clothes I did not recognise, starched dress-shirts, blazers with mock crests loose over her narrow shoulders, and I would carry her to the bed, and she would still be sleeping when I left for my seminar the following morning.

You tell me the sadist punishes his victims out of envy; sadism the penalty for betrayals yet to be committed.

When I try to sleep you whisper the power of woman over man is the power of woman to submit to man; to mime a yielding to violence, to reassert power bonds so primitive they are experienced nowhere but in war, and some bad families; how else had jealousy been invented?

As you pulled me deep into yourself you would beg me to call you by many names, imagine a thousand women writhing in concert, your pleasures as if in parallel mirrors indefinitely multiplying.

You liked to play the mugging game. Up the stairs you came dangling your patent grip, whistling in the dark, and I dragged you down into the laundry-hole, muzzling your mouth, lipstick and pencils and compacts spilling over the floor, and you bit and scratched until I was rough with you.

Later in the harsh light of the inner bathroom, fingering your bruises as if putting the last touches to your make-up.

The exams drew closer, I left the flat almost every day for the Institute, your disappearances more frequent and unpredictable, and on the afternoons when I returned to find you having just woken I would draw my fist from my pocket, and you scratched and pried at each finger until I opened my palm, snuffling the pills down without water, and on the night after the last exam I waited until they had taken hold before driving out towards the airport.

II

To wake each morning in familiar surroundings belies the journey we have taken down into the fathoms of the night.

We do not seem to have travelled for each port appears the same, and when each morning we wake in a strange room, as we do on this last journey across Europe, we are taught again how far we travel, and how fragile the diurnal light, a freshwater harbour beside a measureless ocean, but we are cursed to pace these narrow quays, unsleeping landlubbers, afraid to trust to the winds.

These days every hotel looks the same. We travel but arrive always at the same port.

The place itself seemed comfortable enough when we ascended last night in the leather-padded escalator, a plush bar, stuccoed walls, Delftware at tasteful intervals, but we will not be going down now again for a while.

Our mansard room has a low ceiling, and no view to speak of, and smells faintly of naphthalene, but we are far enough here from the dull riot of Dam Square and at this hour there is little noise other than the fitful mewing of the gulls across the canals.

She assures me this could not be the case, and yet she has a sense she has visited this place before, and at a time perhaps when she hardly cared to know her whereabouts.

The room itself is mercifully spare. Along one side are

fitted cupboards with painted porcelain handles, beside the window a small glass-topped writing desk under a mirror imbricated with primitive Surinamese motifs, in the corner a french fireplace; in the hearth, a spray of thistles.

If there was not scaffolding up to the gables we would be able to look out from our bed over the Prinsengracht to the tower of the Westerkerk where Rembrandt who advised artists never to travel lies buried in an unmarked grave.

But our sole view is that of an undistinguished reproduction hung opposite the bed, one of those inconspicuous and unexceptionable works whose decorative nullity is so peculiarly apt to punctuate the longeurs of hotel walls, but in this light I can discern only that the subject is a still life, and the prevailing tone dark green.

I think it must be difficult to die here. In this city on a floating island in a dead sea. On unebbing water suspended from water and the moon between sluices and ring-dykes. Dying is too natural for such a place.

If I close my eyes I still see the jerking reel of the journey, tired prospects spooling out beyond the train. The small towns with their avenues of linden trees, salvage-yards rank with milkweed, poplars shadowing the roads, and then towards evening the low polders, tidy houses with scrolled shutters backing on to the tracks, windowsills clustered with gezellig.

A landscape glazed against its age, indifferent to the past traffic of sudden expulsions, forced marches, cattle-trains; the same plains her ancestors would have crossed, peddling and fiddling their way out of the black forests of Bohemia and Lithuania, wandering the rutted highways in their clogs until they reached the sea, and the old lepronzenberg of Amsterdam from whose narrow gables they would have stared down in wonder upon the satin and lace of their Sephardi kinsmen drifting below between palazzo stoops in their gilded pleasure-barges.

When I can no longer pretend to sleep she comes and nestles on my side of the carriage we have kept to ourselves with her grips and magazines over every other seat, and she reads me articles she has saved, on Punk Rose's small-screen debut, on the strikes, the environmental crisis; strange girl, she worries I am losing touch.

When we arrived after nightfall at the terminus it was still warm, the windows of the taxi open as we passed down Spuistraat, from the streets the breath of low revelry, spilled lager and hashish smoke blending with the vapours of the tideless Amstel, some teenagers in torn shirts stumbling by in the darkness, one reaching over to steady himself against the idling car, another with boodshot eyes holding up a bottle to toast a night they would not remember; as the car moved on the boy losing his balance, the group staggering off like a pantomime horse into this swinish Venice of the North where the canals are less devious and every day is stale carnival and the maze of alleys only perplexing to the drunk.

Before leaving Kassel I had hoped to visit Schloss Wilhelmslöe to view the monochrome breakfast-piece by Pieter Claesz and a rare vanitas by Willem Van Aelst of which I possessed a small etching she would later steal and sell to one of the dealers on the Portobello Road.

The first day had been too ashen and overcast for a proper estimation of the pictures, we decided to return in more candid light. On our second visit we had found the drive to the castle impeded by a throng of young enthusiasts who had arrived in coaches to view the unveiling of the Duplex Sequence by Foley which was to form the centrepiece of the Documenta Art-Fair, as we came closer it became apparent that this blockage had been aggravated by the added presence of strikers, the latter marching in the opposite direction under wide banners in the shape of Deutschmarks, at the vanguard a small column of Bavarians in national dress; a certain fractiousness had already begun to sour the impasse; marshals interposed between the two groups had been out-jockeyed, from the narrowing gap Goth-haired youths finger-gestured and bayed, and when a trio of hotheads jostled one of the Bavarians and his polished saxtuba to the ground we thought it prudent to abandon the expedition and returned down the castle road into the town.

If we have had a poor night, and we have had five in succession now, we take a Seconal each and slip into a shallow half-sleep until the boy comes with the lunch-trolley and draws back the curtains to the barred light through the scaffolding and the gulls over the canals; the muted chimes of the Westerkerk tower, the trilling of cycle bells.

With the strikes the city is quiet. No trams running down Raadhuistraat, no barges along the Prinsengracht; through the pollarded lime trees the deserted decks of house-sloops; outside the canal-front cafés the tables almost empty.

I do not dare leave her alone, and she is still too frail for the walk down to the Rijksmuseum; she has mislaid the postcards from the lobby; I try to distract her with parodies of my slide-room lecturers.

As our eyes are still too weak for reading during these quiet afternoons we have little choice but to occupy ourselves in the contemplation of the unassuming still life opposite the bed. It has always been my practice to view pictures by natural illumination only, though here the reproduction is of such indifferent quality and the light that falters through the web of scaffolding and pollarded branches so broken and pale that I use the lamp which to obviate collateral shadowing I have placed at a median to the vertex of the canvas.

I had hoped that the hall porter might have secured a photograph of the original from the Rijksprentenkabinet, but he has been unable to gain an audience with Dr Vonde, who remains a virtual prisoner of the pickets.

Draping my head with a puce napkin I resort to my impression of Lisa Jardine.

'Though an initial inspection reveals that there is no overt disaggregation between the objects clustered on the table-top, the composition may be divided nonetheless into three distinct and discrete theatres of focus, the natural inclination of the eye to travel from left to right being mimed by the shaft of light from an undisclosed source falling first on the left-hand side of the table, a bowl of ripe fruit and oyster shucks lying loosely over the damask cloth around a paper cornet overflowing with roughly ground pepper; in the middle passage a plain blomglas, unfluted and uninflected, supporting a single white madonna lily and a wilting rose, to the foreground long white Gouda pipes, still thinly smoking; in the final third, the light illuminates a polished pewter flagon, a fallen roemer glass, some broken bread.

When we look more closely we begin to find other details; a toad in the shadows; flies on the fruit; a pearl, or is it dew, in the dark crevice of a hastily dropped napkin.

Like botanists with natural specimens, it is the practice of art historians first to describe, and then to classify, but I will dispense with such taxonomical finesse and only observe that though the work would conventionally be catalogued as a 'breakfast-piece', in the seventeenth century the Dutch word ontbijt signified a light repast taken at any hour of the day or night, and the oyster, far from being an emblem of prodigality or the vita voluptaria, was a staple of the lowest kitchen, together with asparagus, salmon and the flounder; in a trencherman age when a banquet would seem Lenten if it did not boast oxheads of Rhenish, Gouda greened with the juice of sheep's dung, venison, fricadel, hung beef, hotchpots, trussed swans, such a slight fare as we are presented with here would seem modest to the point of invisibility.

I will not linger upon the dry foundations of the composition, nor upon the sly gradation of the palette, other than to register that the former effects a paradoxical and precarious balance between the intimate and the monumental while the latter descends the chromatic scale from rust through seven hues of olive to brine and yet remains suffused by an even and temperate luminosity whose constancy specifies coldness but whose density resonates warmth.

As to the pedant's trumpery of date and attribution: in the absence of an identifiable signature, ident or monogram, clues are contained in the minute detailing of the thoraxes and wings of the flies on the fruit, and in the precise and dispassionate modelling of the horns and ridge on what is visible of the anterior of the toad, this handling refusing all fashionable Flemish drama, exhibiting a naturalist exactitude which must imply a connection with the circle of Ambrossius Bosschert the Elder of Middleberg where in the last decade of the sixteenth century the master oculists Johannes and Zacharias Jansen had developed the mikroskopen lenses enabling local artists to achieve a novel and unique proximity to natural minutiae; the individual conception of the work would seem to indicate the manner of Bosschert's earliest follower, one Cornelius Tromp, of whom little is known other than the artist visited London in 1604 where he attended a performance of Othello, as is attested to in an entry in the diary of the antiquary Nicholas Fossard, and died from the quartan fever in Amsterdam in the summer of 1605 while delivering a flower-piece to a Sephardi spice-merchant.

The interest in a work such as this resides precisely in what is absent from the composition, and the rationale of that exclusion, for you will remember that it was the practice of the near contemporaries of our artist to deploy scientific naturalism to appease the curiosity of their patrons by delighting always in the exotic and the rare, and if they could not always depict novel natural specimens and wonders they would at least show familiar ones by means of newfangled illusionisms, and yet against the livid background of this prevailing taste for the exquisite and the intricate, the domestic simplicity of this homely table-top appears nothing less than remarkable; while his peers sought out the uncommon textures and tones of the exotic fruits from the markets of Antwerp, sweet-rinded cumquats from Cathay, setiferous madagascals, pepos nobbly as sea-urchins, dark pomelos and oranges from the Levant, our frugal Cornelius sets before us rustic berries and ungarnished fruits, black plums and apples whose worm-pits and contusions would suggest they had only just been garnered from the orchard floor.

Although the indifferent quality of the reproduction precludes too intimate an estimation of the brushwork there is evident relish in the fluid handling of the viscous residue within the scattered oyster shucks, but again belied by the compositional spareness of the few discarded husks which seem deliberately to shun the ready abundance of his native maritime provinces so deftly celebrated by his fellow guildsmen who could realise the ornamental properties of such modest fare as common dabs, bloaters and cured herring, and represent a lobster with as much care and character as if it were the Prince of Orange.

Only the cornet of ground pepper appears as a prodigal and alien presence amongst the other victuals, a miniature horn-of-plenty rendered with a sensuous and trembling brush; a paper calyx dispensing its pollen.

For the palate of that age had been delicately unsettled by those spices which returned in the convoys of East-Indiamen running the gauntlet of British warships and privateers around the Cape of Good Hope from Malacca and Malay, and these were the years when pepper was the object of wild speculation under the flighty cupolas and arcades of the new bourse across the Rokin and when the wharves and warehouses of the Oostindisch Huis were swollen with the greatest concentration of lucre in all Europe; pearls, rubies; dressed Persian silks, Japanese lacqueur, indigo, sappanwood; ceylon candy; the garners and attics waist-high in cinammon, cloves, ground nutmeg and mace.

But our temperate Cornelius will not permit such cornucopian freight to capsize his concise allegory, and so he shows us only a simple wilting rose, a broken lily, rude Gouda pipes still smoking thinly. And such restraint while his contemporaries vied to delight their patrons with subtle and profuse bouquets of the most fashionable blooms, offsetting humble native flora with grape-hyacinths, fritillaries, their bowed heads like lampshades, anemones, columbines, streaked viceroy tulips of such absolute rarity that a single bulb would have been traded for an entire farm.

More undemanding patrons may have tolerated the pipes, but then only in a smoking ensemble, with tapers, resting on cool blue Ming.

Then there is the closing passage, in an age when drinking was a matter of some ceremony, and in a land of ornate toasting-rituals, such emphatic reserve; the broken bread, upturned roemer glass; the pewter flagon.'

You say it is the scene of a crime, all left as it was, waiting for forensic.

The pulled cloth, the toppled glass, the table hastily abandoned; but what disturbed the eater; to what judgement has he so suddenly been summoned?

You say it reminds of waking to the ruins of last night's pleasures; of a deep attachment unwillingly forgone.

I opened my eyes, your coat no longer slung over the chair.

I did not wait for your return, but took a taxi directly to Schiphol, and another from Heathrow through the last of the rush-hour traffic to the flat.

In his bed Crispian was asleep with flu; your fallen clothes and toiletries undisturbed.

It was too early for the Ozbar; my palm against the bell-buttons until the main door was buzzed open, but on the upper landing no response from within.

It was dusk as I reached the mansion block above Marylebone High Street; men in suits with briefcases and shopping bags hurrying past the art-deco entrance-portico; the bright lobby empty.

In the passages above the high atrium I could not find the light-switches, down through the dark funnels a trail of pounding bass leading finally to the door with the hand-of-Fatima knocker.

Along the inner corridor, the end-partition ajar. The sitting-room emptied of furniture, only two wardrobe-sized speakers; a black leather sofa jutting out across the middle of the floor like a giant pinball-flipper.

It takes a moment in the dimness to separate out the thick twist of bodies locked together over the sofa. The girl is naked, kneeling forward, against the shrivelled wings of her breasts.

Her body slowly rocking as if in an invisible sling, a man straddling her from behind, with each thrust his pale untanned buttocks clenching; on the other side, Amir, grasping her head in towards him by the hair, his face thrown up towards the ceiling, the skin pulling back from his gums into a fixed rictus.

In the deafening bass, every movement a sort of agony; like machinists at work on the shop-floor, their weighted movements trapped by the din into the irrevocable rhythm of ritual.

In the kitchen, over the long stripped-pine table, an

old-fashioned clothes-rack hung with copper pans, ladles, skillets; alone by the dust-glazed hob you sit close over the square of blackened foil, as if working a sampler.

And when you look up you smile casually, as if you had been expecting me; without speaking, you follow through the atrium into the sodium-glare of the night.

III

Outside the streets are loose with summer again. I had not noticed until today. The lighter swish of the traffic beyond the flats, the smell of frying floating up from the back-yard of the Aphrodite. The sudden emptiness of the afternoons.

And later there will be the cooing of the pigeons, the calling of children from the green. Tonight I will listen for them, and you will remember perhaps the seasons of the city passing one into another seamless as two seas meeting; the darkness into this sullen light.

Until evening I will play music and read the newspapers as I always do now. No one bothers me here. I rise for the lunchtime news without fear of the post. When I draw the curtains, the blank street, undistracting.

But today the sour heat has brought out the Cypriot grocer, he stands watching the fruit ripen under the tricolour-striped awning; somewhere behind on the estate, the jangle of the ice-cream van.

On days like this in the old flat I would open all the windows, as wide as the burglar-locks allowed. And you would squat cross-legged under the curtains trembling in the breeze.

You liked to stare at the swirling dust, the cat lounging out on the unsafe terrace. You might have cried out of course,

123

but that could always be explained later. Even before I had stopped going into the Institute I would lock the Chubb on the inside door, disconnect the telephone.

Those last months we never left the flat. In the darkness I would hear her scratching at her breasts, at the windows, the water always running with the door closed so as not to wake me.

Sometimes I would sit beside the bath and hold her as she shuddered in the scalding water; when her pee disturbed the surface of the water and she could not hide it she would begin to laugh, and I would have to kiss her to stop her teeth chattering; every day her tone lightening; mustard, amber, clear honey.

She was usually at her best in the mornings. She liked to clean then. She would tire herself out on the surfaces in the kitchen. When all the Wettex were worn through I had to stop her using her hands.

When the mornings were hot I would not let her clean, she would hide in the washing-room, and I would find her sweating on the lid of the deep white coffin of a freezer I had bought to garner our unseasonal hibernation.

Sometimes I would return and find the curtains all closed, and the taps running in the dark, and there would be a strange peace to the place like walking at night into a garden where water flows.

And now when I score those final hours for the hidden music of their deceit I hear nothing but the lisp of her breathing; the worst phases of withdrawal were through by then, her torn synapses slowly beginning to heal.

But when I went out that morning I had not overlooked the usual safeguards. I had gone through the pockets of my jackets for cash and spare keys, disconnected the telephone and locked it in the desk, twice-turned the Chubb on the inner door.

It was hot that day. She was sitting in the washing-room

on the cool lid of the freezer, the smoke still not cleared from her last cigarette lit off the hob, her knees bunched up under her faded T-shirt, one of my father's old handkerchiefs in a sweaty ball under the wash-pinched sleeve.

She was reading again, a small book, balanced in her lap. I remember thinking how still she was, a knight in effigy bowed over his marble scripture. When I had asked from the doorway what flavours of soup and ice-cream she wanted, she had not looked up, but she had thought about it.

'Cookie and pecan . . . and vanilla.'

At first of course it was impossible to believe she would be gone for long. The flat was still too full of her. There would be a binge, a penitent return. We would begin all over again, as we had before. I used the time to sleep; I enjoyed having the bed to myself for once.

Then there were the weeks of waiting. I never made calls for fear she would be trying to get through. I kept all the doors open, and the windows closed, so I would not miss the ringing, and kept lifting the receiver to check the line was still connected.

All sounds that might distract from the ringing I suppressed. No running water, the curtains closed against the wash of the traffic. At night I placed the telephone beside the bed, but still I feared I would sleep through the ringing and stayed up drinking coffee and reading old copies of art-historical journals in the poor light.

After a week of this I began to lose my sense of the scale of sounds. A sifting percussion of rustlings and drips played through all the rooms. Sometimes I would think I heard scratchings on the pane, the click and fizz of her lighter, the buzzer down the hall, a taxi pulling up outside. I would draw back the curtain, and look down into the empty street.

Occasionally calls did come through. Immediately I heard the ringing I had already discounted them. I told the caller it was a bad time, no point in phoning back, I would be out later.

I hovered between sounds and the ghosts of sounds; the drag of the outer door against uncollected mail; the distant moan of a dog waiting on the return of its master.

Cookie and pecan . . . and vanilla.

Sometimes as I honed to one of the sounds, trampling over books and plastic methadone beakers, I would meet her face in the low light, pale as thinned milk, but that curtained gloom saved me from her hair in the plughole, her blood on the sheets, her little smear on the side of the bowl.

Her talent had always been for the unoriginal in its purest form, her genius to make of the ordinary an immaculate mystery. Even in her final degradation she could still enchant the world quite out of its character.

Early one morning amidst all these flounderings and minor hallucinations the telephone began to ring, loud as an alarm bell, from the wrong side of the bed. In my anguish she had once more framed me in a scene of absolute derivation. A telephone ringing in the night, a desperate man tracking the flex through the undergrowth of a dark apartment.

The voice was slightly breathless, an old-time voice that no longer bothered to identify itself, Foley.

'You'll never believe who just arrived.' Already I was reaching for clothes. I would go and bring her back before she knew we had spoken.

'He just called from the airport.'

I could see her shivering in a call-box on some desolate estate, the cat in her bag, trying to get through.

'It's Shaman. He's doing clubs now.'

'I'm waiting for a call.'

I put down the receiver.

In time I settled into a vigil, with rules and routines. I would

126

sleep a little in the early afternoon after the last post had come. In the mornings I would sit with the telephone at the top of the stairs down to the hall. By the dull light through the dirty glass I could skim the newspapers, and then put them by for the night; as the weeks passed I became an expert on back-bench revolts, the strikes in Europe, the hostage crisis.

I found I did not miss the cat. Nor did I wonder that she should have taken her and left so much else behind; her address book, clothes, fine-decoration manuals.

Through their blithe indifference they had mirrored each other, with uncanny precision, each a sly imago of the other, never together in the same room.

She had been Sylvie's idea of course, though I had fed and watered her, and if I forgot she went hungry. We had driven all the way down to a rectory on the Devon moors, and after much cooing deliberation she had picked her out.

She had been taken with the filigree of white on her upper legs, but had not cared for the name, Cancan. She said it sounded like a cheap scent. It was true there was nothing of petticoats or high-stepping about the molten way the creature slunk between things; she wanted to call her Cunard, then it was Candy (short for Candace) but if she answered at all it was only to Cancan, and so we stuck with it in the end.

It was not long before rooms were closed to her, first Sylvie's closet, then the bedroom, the bathrooms, until she had only the freedom of the kitchen, and that on sufferance. Being a Mau she was short-haired and trim, but when Sylvie found her hairs on cushions and the duvet she started into a madness of brushing and wiping; one afternoon I had seen her out on the unsafe terrace prodding with a broom towards the edge where the cat was perched; she had forgotten that this was the way Cancan habitually took when she launched herself down on to the pavement.

At first, taking her disappearance for a sorry coincidence, I had continued in the mornings to change her bowls. She was not a mouser, just a carpet cat. It was difficult to picture her out on the streets for long.

With time I became a connoisseur of boredom, like any other hostage. I taught myself to channel-flip, to play with numbers, to smoke again. My thin existence left few new traces in the flat. Some disasters preserve well. I was just the curator now, metaphors my consolation.

In those months I never dreamt of her. I would have old dreams; a stench of cordite, the sick joke of the blast sucking all breath from my lungs, shoppers running down the other side of the street, and someone putting their hand over my eyes.

The day I finally decided to shut the place up and go back to the island I was woken by a familiar voice calling up from the street. I looked through the slit between the drawn curtains, and saw Anna on a motorbike, a black crash-helmet under her arm; at first I tried to sit it out, but when she carried on shouting I weakened and went down and opened the door.

It had been eighteen months since our last fraught encounter, and she had changed again; her shrunken tank-top over toned tattooed arms, close-shaved hair, dyed carotene, a cuneiform razored in above her left temple. She was tanned up to her neck, but her face was studiously pale, and too old for all that now.

She walked from room to room, talking familiarly about people I did not know, with her ungloved hand picking up Sylvie's effects, methadone bottles, odd boots, tortoiseshell compacts, and then dropping them to the floor. I waited on the stairs.

She came down into the dim hall, and stood by the broken dresser. Behind the piercings and the assumed butchness there was a new fear in her, dilating her narrowed cobalt eyes, and for the first time like a sculptor in a quarry I could see Sylvie's precise form inside her, as if still waiting to be freed from the block of stone.

It was as if this fear was the pressure of the Sylvie within her waiting to be born, the serpent slowly slipping its coils, and when she told me in the same casual tone in which she had just been speaking that only a couple of weeks before she had seen Sylvie with Don Luis on the island I did not believe her, and I kept asking her to come up again and share a porro as in the old days, and she pretended not to hear, and lowering her fly-blooded visor she walked slowly back to the motorcycle parked against the spiked iron railings under the terrace where I had always feared the cat might come to harm.

I will go now and have my lunch as usual across the road at the Kleftiko. I never see anyone else eating there, but it stays open after two-thirty while the Aphdrodite next door is always full of local shoppers and businessmen, and there is never a free table when I come down.

The stocky owner has developed the habit of raising his eyes with the pious reproach of a priest observing one fallen from his congregation as I walk past the sea-tinted windows and across to the door of his quiet rival.

Inside the restaurant is divided into a series of cavernous alcoves whose shadowiness is probably more a matter of economy than atmosphere. Over the rustic plastering of the walls hang the usual Taverna bric-à-brac, dusty ceramics, straw donkeys, maps of an undivided Cyprus; a loop tape of Bazuki playing from somewhere behind the bar.

Although I come almost every day now the young waiter always seems surprised when I enter. He smiles weakly and gestures towards the empty row of alcoves. His face is oyster-grey, shadowed by bad nights, and he brings the food to the table with an overdetermined care, as if walking beside a chasm, his bowed gait warped by some unspoken shame. Every day I break my resolve and cannot quite bring myself to come down from the overblown tip I gave on my first visit. I worry about the effect on his morale.

After lunch I stroll up to the newsagent's, but go no further than the Goat and Monkey at the corner of the green beyond which lies that muddle of railway arches and low-rise estates where two of the tectonic plates of the city invisibly meet.

On the other side of this breach lies Rustum's territory. His long-standing residence in Oxford Gardens has tinctured all the surrounding streets between Esmond Square and the arches, and though he has not been seen outside his house for the last three years he still receives local visitors of a certain persuasion and enjoys playing with powerful binoculars, and so I am careful not to venture too close. If she goes to ground there when she is in town as I suspect, and I am sighted from the windows, all my patience will have been wasted.

I keep to this side of the green, walking past the snooker club on the edge of the square which is closed during the day. Sometimes towards evening I have passed and seen the shy waiter from the Kleftiko among those boys loitering outside, and he must be relieved that I do not greet him.

Beyond the green I cut back through the estate to my rooms. With the twin-tower high-rise at one end and the Goat and Monkey being the sort of pub it is the street attracts few visitors. There is the quiet to hope again.

My father has become too deaf to use the telephone, but when I close my eyes I hear only his weakening voice, and when I open my eyes I cannot keep from looking at those parts of the room where his letters lie hidden.

Before I try to write I pull out at random one of the earlier envelopes, the final small ritual I draw across my day.

. . . and you must not be surprised that this disappointment has only been displaced by the additional disappointment of discovering from your last letter that you still remain so wholly preoccupied with the disappearance of Miss Bloom, although I am of course no donaivolo in these matters there may perhaps be some consolation in knowing that I had always considered Miss Bloom rather less remarkable than the pains you expended on her.

It was undeniable she possessed a certain unlearnt grace and poise which quite disguised her ordinariness, and I must confess to knowing few women in whom such qualities remained so precisely artless, and yet her grace was of that variety rarely leavened by charm or natural wit not uncommon in women of her mixed background which exercises its own especial fascination on young men who choose to mistake density for depth, and I could not fail to observe that despite her youth and elegance there was about her a sullen blandness, an element unreactive and almost inanimate at the core of her being, a dark matter annulling that which it attracts, and had I not been obliged to respect the pieties of your infatuation I would of course have wished long before the first symptoms became apparent to share with you my belief that it is always the prerogative of a girl of this type to turn vile, but you may at least be certain that I take no pleasure in having witnessed my predictions vindicated by the years . . .

But it was not the shame of my reclusive obsession, nor the embarrassment of not finding suitable employment since leaving the Institute which had prevented me returning to my father on the island.

I had long understood there was an unspoken covenant. I was to write down the story of which I had yet to hear the ending. I could write nothing in this city haunted by her ghosts, only that diary scrawled in the half-light from which I have built this broken fiction.

ANNA

Caracteres tal vez formados alados
en el papel diáfano del cielo
las plumas de su vuelo

Congora

1990–1991

I

Each day the clínica sends a different nurse. He calls them all by the same name.

She stands in front of his chair, opens the stiff curtains. Below the littered terrace, a slick of rainwater in the drained pool; the rocks under the breakwater blackened by spent bonfires.

He turns his head from the view, and shakes his stick until she understands, and the curtains are closed again.

The catheter runs out from under his sleeve to a syringe on the stool by the chair, the fluid inside the hectic rose of a child's drink; on the arm-rest, the food he has not been able to swallow. She removes the prop-up tray too soon.

Each morning I sit on the cold tiles, my cheek against his pain-thinned leg, his bone fingers through my briny hair; over his damp crotch, the circle of worry-beads like a fallen crown.

I need to be close to him now, his voice fitful, fading in and out like a faraway radio station.

In the shadows he sifts the old stories; the deserts, Cambridge, the return to Jerusalem; through the lumber to a later chapter of his brother's life I had never heard before.

It was only two years since their son had been born in

the holiday villa they had built in imitation of the island house in Jerusalem, and with the Arab armies massing on all three borders Ariane had not wished to risk the journey with Pascal to Nazareth.

That summer Walter had begun teaching music in the UNWRA school on the esplanade above the mosque, and Pascal had driven up in his new Ford Falcon to take photographs of the youth orchestra for the first exhibition he had planned in the former studio on the Jaffa Road.

He arrived in the heat of the afternoon. The classrooms and the three-sided courtyard deserted, all the children up on the hills smoking behind the wild figs, watching for the dust clouds of the Syrian tanks.

As evening came on the streets around the school remained quiet. Fruit lorries and vans and old pick-ups had been confiscated the week before by the army. Through dusk the moan of the curfew bell, the blacked-out windows of houses like the paper epitafio-lanterns which protect the procession candles from the night winds.

All night he sits up with Walter and Geli in the adjoining apartment; the french windows on to the verandah painted over with blue Nili washing-cubes, patrols crossing the esplanade like shoals of fish in an aquarium.

They hunker down under the stone hearth; crouching, she brings wine, bowls of pistachios, sugared almonds, water-melon seeds; peach-tinctured tobacco-cakes for the softly bubbling narghile.

At dawn he opens the door; down in the dim valley a single Mig jet flying across the maize fields; the impact blast short and muted as a match being blown out.

Throughout the morning the cinema-hoarding trucks circling the square; on the high double billboards the faces of Nasser, Azizi, Hussein, smeared with faeces; tannoys announcing that East Jerusalem had fallen, and the Arab tank-columns lay burning in the deserts.

The children did not come down from the hills; he followed the army convoy back to Jerusalem.

The streets below Mamilla like a carnival of penitents, the fellahin women wailing and tearing their hair, the old men shaking their fists at the sky, on every corner shebab from the east staring at the fair-haired women, wolf-whistling, under the ramparts a teeming sea of black robes and hats, Orthodox and Hasidi pressing through the gates of the old city to touch the one surviving wall of the temple.

At the studio on the Jaffa Road he picks up his long-lens Cannon, his smallest Pentax, his hamper of film, and without stopping for a late lunch at the house drives on towards the southern border.

Through the ring-road around Tel Aviv, the ancient port and quays hidden by the new apartment buildings and earlier settler tenements, beyond along the beach highway above mazes of barakiat a long tangle of aerials and roof-top water-tanks and sahra-shelters over the gleaming indifference of the sea.

Avoiding the army roadblocks on the lower roundabouts, he heads north, across country through orchard lanes and wadis to Beersheba.

Over the desert the way marked only by rusted petrol cans and drifting tumbleweed, through wind-rippled sands he came to the corrugated-iron police post where he had sheltered from the rains all those years ago, and from the heights the plain as if covered by remnants of the old crude-oil roads, broken black lines leading like semaphore across the blank scrolls of the sahool; the burnt-out hulks of the tanks and personnel-carriers like rotten teeth, and above the wheeling vultures.

Over on the horizon the dust-trail of a slowly approaching jeep, through the wheezing grid of the air-conditioning the tart smell of burnt flesh.

He leaves the Falcon behind the low tel, hides the Cannon

and hamper, and walks up among the dunes, the higher slopes sown with crumpled and charred florets, over this garden of buried iron, dried tears of oil, the flick-stains of a fountain pen.

On the final ridge what lay embedded in the sands seemed not to have fallen but to have grown like the first shoots of a ruined harvest; singed webbing, boots, helmets, severed hands.

The dead still held their stations, disposed over the black shells like models in an anatomical class, a gunner on the turret as if simply pausing to pose for his camera, over the blackened ledge his fallen offal tidily arrayed; his skinless companion a white mummy of cartilage and muscle groping the darkening sky, and below there were those ranging their guns under the caterpillar tracks which had not saved them, their crouching postures melted and moulded over the iron notches, and others down in the wadi scored into the sandbanks like ideograms of their own fate.

In the carriers beyond all had been pecked clean down to their skeletons, and in the ditches he saw fresher bodies prone and kneeling with their hands behind their heads, only their eyes and cheeks gone, and when he had finished his film he walked back towards the car, the soldiers in the jeep shouting at him in dog-Hebrew and waving their assault-rifles and as he started across the plain he levelled his long-lens blindly behind until the dirt clouds concealed the view back to the ridge.

Driving back along the path he had travelled so many years before he knew again the strange peace of the desert at night where all is preserved as in the memory of his one God, and as monuments turned to dust and cities were lost under the waters all he had seen that evening had always already been there, and there would remain until the end of the ages.

The first fingers of dawn over the dome of the conquered city. He parks in front of the locked gates to the drive.

Outside the high wall, a police car, an ambulance; he looks down through the olive terrace to see if there has been trouble among the barakiyat, but it is dark there.

Through the hall and the manzul all the lights are on, and he calls her name, and when there is no reply from upstairs he walks out by the kitchen door.

From the vine-covered verandah, he can see white coats and navy-blue jackets at the edge of the pool, and two men are walking with a stretcher from the tessellated surround to the side of the house, the others staring at the seamless water as if waiting for an answer, and as he runs down he is held back by the Sephardi policeman.

Over his shoulder, standing up on the lit verandah, the maid; the small boy wrapped in a yellow blanket, and the boy is sleeping.

When they understand who he is they open the back of the ambulance. She had been found by the maid floating face-down in the shallow end, and he kisses her white lips, and her bloated cheeks, and the water-flies and chlorine from her eyes.

Seeing the lights the refugees from the barakiyat have wandered up through the terrace, and when the elders heard that the woman who had clothed and fed them through many hard winters had drowned in the pool of water they had never seen, they knelt on the ground, and wept like children.

The leader asked the policeman who had killed the Sitt, and the man held up an arm to the sky, and pointed a finger, and made a full circle in the lightening air.

From that morning his days would be an enduring dark-ness. He had looked up and seen the moon stolen from his sky.

He could no longer live in the house. Before it was

sold he moved into the new top floor of the King David Hotel, his rooms above the suite where he had first photographed her.

As she had once looked over the city, her hunched shoulders the stumps of lost wings, so his little boy peered out at the grey walls and the golden dome.

Each morning he dangles oranges from the window, the dome a giant orange-squeezer.

By spring the house was sold. They moved to Beirut, to a villa at the other end of the headland from the small apartment which Anton and Anastasia still shared.

She thinks I tire him. After she has helped him eat his yoghurt and chopped fruit from the prop-up tray, she wheels him through to the bedroom.

I walk down from the terrace over the sand-flooded lawns to the beach, a humid mist on the hills, the damp grit clinging to my shoes; over the wash and the hum of the carretera, the barking of the chuchos among the empty summer villas.

Above the security arc-lights, the Sandeman hoarding, the silhouette of the cape and wide-brimmed hat, a black hole in the sepia of the autumn dusk.

I look out beyond the breakwater, the view from Rose's window already as faint and remote as the passing tanker lights far across the straits.

Between the lower scrub-reaches of Laurel Canyon, white villas perched like tree-houses, the lines of street-lights below converging like a painter's perspective-grid to an infinite horizon, towards the invisible sea the ziggurats of Century City, and higher up the winking headlamps of the cars of the courting couples parked in the lay-bys off Mulholland to enjoy the same view.

I had met Rose again during my last month in London when I had broken my self-imposed curfew to attend the

Royal Première at the Odeon in Leicester Square of a period farce in which she had played the soubrette; I had been invited by Reaper's American partner, the stage Viking, Michael-Jon.

Before the film I had joined them at their new house in Church Street, the lower storeys still being renovated and without lighting, his Cheshire-Cat grin suspended in the shadows; he seemed to read my mind for throughout the evening he would tell me about nothing else but how that week he was to have his teeth 'de-whitened'.

Under the glow of the girandoles in the hall, lengths of copper piping, the livid scrawls of Basquiats and Harings leaning against the unpainted walls, and beyond reposing on an empire couch with a silk dressing-gown over his suit Reaper not acknowledging my presence, and continuing to talk about his love of greyhounds to one of those figureheads coated in gold flakes which the Muisca Indians had cast as sacrifices into their mountain lakes, her hips flexing under the flickering lamé as she sauntered out of the shadows for an air-kiss on her way up to the floor with electricity to make her final preparations for the evening ahead.

Reaper would never refer back to those months two years before when I had called regularly at the flat in the small square off Westbourne Grove, and having made his fortune as the first supplier of Ecstasy to an emerging market had already diversified into contemporary art and latterly the film business; on the telephone the month before he had spoken vaguely of my 'doing some surgery on a script', but that evening I must have been invited as a late stand-in for whoever had dropped out at the last minute as Rose's walker.

Before the film Rose stood in line with the rest of the cast and the producers and their wives as the princess walked along the puce carpet in a similar but longer gold-lamé gown, and when Rose curtsied it was as if she was looking up at herself in the mirror.

The charity gala was held at the hotel opposite Bush House on Upper Regent Street, and on arriving Reaper had disappeared into one of the service-passages on the trail of a bell-boy, and Michael-Jon was lost among the crush around the princess, and irritated at being ignored Rose had insisted on being taken home early, and I had escorted her in a black cab to her old flat off the Fulham Road where she still kept a room to use during her brief visits to London.

From the side-door I followed her up the narrow stairway to the first-floor sitting-room, over the kitchen-range along the inner wall piles of unwashed plates, garlic-strings, shrivelled fruit, and I do not remember what we talked about as we finished the bottle of open Chablis on the table, and from the sofa I had watched her hang up her dress in its polythene sheath with a slow and meticulous deliberation as if securing an article of nuclear waste, and after a drunken and perfunctory rut over the end of the bed we had lain as still and close as a double burial under the cold sheets, and when I woke she had already left for the airport.

But here in the villa in the canyon she turns in early, and like a long-married couple I wait reading while she performs her convoluted ablutions in the marble en-suite, and from her mucus of cream through the steam she emerges like a creature newly born, and she comes to bed in a sports-bra and an algae-mask and lies face up beneath the sky-at-night ceiling to avoid creases, and will only let me touch her hand, and I cannot sleep for the droning of the humidifiers.

In the mornings she is woken by her Chinese trainer, below the whirr of the blender as he prepares her fruit and soya-milk breakfast, and afterwards he drives her to the gym down on Melrose, and too tired to work I try to sleep again until she returns to dress for lunch.

In the afternoons still numbed by the Seconal I wander blinking through the shuttered temple to her vanity, the scallop-pink dados to bring up the flush in her high cheeks, chartreuse swags to complement her pupils, along the gallery through the venetian blinds, wands and plumes of brilliant light over the warm cream runner; avoiding the flies and the heat in the glassed-in pigeonnier where she believes I spend my days writing the screenplay which will immortalise her I shelter on the massage-table in her long closet where heavy curtains have been hung to prevent the colours fading, and the crowded hangers block out the remaining glare.

If she made me forget you for a moment it was by never letting me see beyond her immaculate surfaces and the fine protocol by which she measured our days. When she is not on the telephone to her agent or her actress friends whom I am never allowed to meet she asks me to define my love for her, and I tell her lust is deductive in that it subsumes the individual into the universal, and love is inductive for in the individual the lover finds his universe, his grains of sand, his canopy of stars. She would never know that always I was writing you into her role.

Through the thick curtains I peer down on to the sundeck, forgotten cocktail glasses, now filled with unseasonal rain.

The clothes against the inner wall are all black, some limp and shrivelled as flayed skins, some slight and frail as shades; above on the shelf the light jewellery in the lacquer cases rattling like beetles in a matchbox; the bosses and lozenges of the patent handbags; the glass amphora of the perfume with which she crosses her three pulse-points before she leaves the house like holy water before going out among the damned.

At the furthest end of her nightclub selection, latex sheaths like poured black chocolate, under the rubber

147

dresses a frass of baby-powder; calf-hide jodhpurs, moiré shifts like seaweed slicked by the tide, glacé hipsters, pearlised bodygloves; Lycra catsuits with the dull sheen of body-bags.

In my unwritten screenplay she strode through the parties and the clubs like one of the leathermen from Barbarella, shellacked surface hiding absolute void, she has not been born, and therefore cannot die, but when in the enchantment of the shadows you rise up in her precious skins they were fruit ripe to bursting, your body viscous as unshed tears, in your black flanks the reflected world faint as the mist-lights which our island folklore believes are the spirits of unborn children.

There was always a point when you no longer knew whether everything was pure invention, and if this invention was not truer than yourself, and after her late lunches I would pretend to have just come down from the pigeonnier, and as she spoke to her long-standing actor boyfriend in England and her girlfriends and scrawled in her diary with her hypodermic pen she would always undress with great care, examining for stains, folding the suits back on to the rosewood hangers with the concentrated reverence of a maid dressing her mistress, and standing in her stockings and sheer-body in front of the tall mirrors she would look at me reproachfully if I did not begin to take her through the latest love scene from the fictitious screenplay, but before the action was resolved her stylist would arrive to prepare her for the evening.

In the pigeonnier she cannot see her precise reflection in the untinted glass, and if on cooler and overcast days I remained writing at the desk she would distract me by reading aloud in her plummy pre-war radio voice, favourite passages from Waugh and Wodehouse, and I would come down to meet her staring green eyes in the cheval over the dim bluff of her naked haunches as in the Rockby Venus, and if I made to fuck her she would banish me outside the door with some recent magazine-spread of herself, and out of politeness I would play along and hog-wimper in the narrow hall, her body tossing like a drenched puppy as she brought herself off with the remote, the reflections of the random channel-flips over the cream walls and sky-at-night ceiling like a flood of toxic water.

She makes love like a taxi-dancer, her rhythm precise, unlingering, with the perpetual indifference of the machine to its use and users, under the even massage-lotion sheen the oiled pistons of her limbs flexing and churning in the mirrors surrounding the bed; when she had finished and lay smoking in my arms it was with a certain dulled relief as if after a final hard-won take, and I had asked her why she did not want to take more time, and she had replied that her last director had told her 'when people think they've seen enough of something, but there's more, no change of shot, they react in a curiously livid way', and she would push the basalt ashtray to the corner of the table and wait for my sweat to dry and nestle against my narrow chest so silently I could not hear her breathing until the first bars of Love Is All You Need announced the arrival of the stylist who would prepare her for the evening to come.

That was the year Gervase was opening his bespoke-tailoring franchises in Palm Springs and La Hoya, and down on the patio we would eat the soft-shell crab he had brought up from the Ivy, and he would amuse himself indulging in savage and elaborate critiques of the cut of my suit, and after the corkscrew-haired stylist had left with her sports-bag we would wait for Rose to make her Sunset Boulevard descent, and sometimes if it was a grand industry party or a première others from the local British colony would collect in the hall, agents, journalists, actors, and Reaper would come disguised as a film-producer in a satin baseball cap and matching jacket like an outsize jockey, with Michael-Jon who had grown a languid fringe and affected an Oxbridge drawl, and together we would drive in their Range Rover out to Santa Monica, or Malibu, or up into the hills, but thankfully she would never stay long, and having timed her entrance past the photographers she would work the room with deft economy and leave without saying her goodbyes, and always when we were alone together as on those long drives through the wide avenues lined with tall kotah palms and florid gates it was as if a great dark screen had come down between the moment and what had gone before, and she would never speak of the small stitch of time we had once shared.

In this respect the ugly are the same as the beautiful, they get tired of being looked at all the time, and she would strut down the steps above the crowd as if putting out cigarettes, and between the jostling rows still waiting to enter she would keep her poise like a gimbal in a storm, and when we got home if she had drunk too much she would put on her blonde bob-wig and do her doe-eyed impression of the princess, and I would want to be rough and dirty with her, but she would insist I film her with the camcorder, and though we turned on all the uplights and the floorlamps and the downlights in the perpetual dusk of the play-backs always she would seem lost and draggled like a drowned doll.

The only occasion she referred to our shared past was the night before I had finally contrived an excuse for leaving when we had gone out alone to a former gay discothèque in West Hollywood to watch a fashionable illusionist, and as each number began she would explain the technique, the double switches, the midget hidden in the secret compartment, the twins, and after the show had ended we had waited as ahead a thin old man with a cravat and an ivory cane was slowly escorted up the aisle by a skinhead in torn jeans, and as the pair had passed we had heard the boy laugh like a hyena and declare 'Beauty is a superstition, admit beauty, you admit God, Truth and the whole juju of metaphysics', and later in the car when she had asked me if that had not been the dandy friend who always used to come to the café on the High Street I had lied and told her Palgrave was still playing Oscar Wilde in his long-running fringe-act in Notting Hill Gate.

After weeks of being kept awake by the drone of the humidifier, I had abandoned all attempts to write during the day, and in the afternoon if I had tried to sleep while she was out at lunch I would be woken by the rumpus down in the hall when Reaper and Michael-Jon brought in Hispanic boys from Echo Park and paraded about in her sling-backs and ball-gowns.

The evening after the illusionist I had resolved to tell her my father had fallen ill and I would have to return to the island, but had not found the right moment, and in the middle of the night the telephone began ringing, and when she had heard the Spanish voice she had put down the receiver presuming it was just another wrong number, and it was only after the second call that I recognised the hissing dialect of our island; my lie had become a curse.

And an hour later on the freeway towards LAX, the drunken Korean driver asking me where I was flying mis-heard the name of our island, and turned to me with a knowing leer.

'Ah Manilla,' he said. 'Much pretty girl.'

That morning for the last time I was leaving my city of smoke and mirrors.

II

The night they took my father back to the clínica the second time I could not sleep and walked out beyond the breakwater to watch the flocks flying south, but the skies above the estuary were empty.

I took the path above the reed-shallows and sluice-ducts towards the marina, the beaches beyond the breakwater overlooked by the pool-decks and solaria below the new hotels, the steep banks planted with agave and spindly palms under the blank façades of the pueblo developments and unfinished time-shares. Down on the last turn before the bay on the mist-blurred promenade, the festive flicker of an ambulance light.

Each week in the island newspapers there were reports of clubbers overdosing and drug-related murders, sleeping-bags washed up on the beach like giant pupae stuffed with drowned men, skeletons in the lime-pits of the sierra, decayed bodies in the sewers under Bellamar; most of the dead were never identified.

Down from the headland to the wide shingle across the bay below San Roque, most of the clubs already closed for the season, between the ruined chiringuitos the sand arenas and poured-concrete floors strewn with crushed cans and plastic fronds, around the boarded-up bars small huddles of rough-sleepers; under the cowls of their burnouses, the faint glow of cigarettes cupped against the wind across the straits; up on the carretera, the roadside signs bright above the beach, Hypnosis, Spectrum, Amnesia; on the far side of the bay over the cove where we used to meet when the bar closed on the square, his name in bleary neon dangling from the claws of a soaring eagle.

Tired from the climb up over the damp sands, I catch my breath at the water-fountain under the orange trees; along the narrow square where there had once been tapaterías and marisquerías, the florid doorways of the shut-up surf shops and karaoke clubs; where our bar had been, a windowless wall patterned with phosphorescent beaks and wings, through the entrance the waving arms of the boys in bandanas and Day-Glo T-shirts, and on a raised mixing-table, a priest giving sacrament, Shaman bowing to the throb of the base beat, a glassine sweat over his shaved head and hollow cheeks, his watery eyes like over-easy eggs.

Hearing my hissing accent, the tattooed doorman looking dismissively at my ripped sneakers, and closing the door in my face. I rap hard on the spy-slit; he pushes me down among the empty bottles in the alley.

The following day when I woke it was almost noon; I telephoned the clínica, the nurse told me he was sleeping.

All afternoon a bitter levante wind gusting spray against the lower walls, rippling the sand on the dead lawns, stirring the self-sown creepers under the rusted satellite-dish, scattering the petals from the last of the geraniums the nurses had been watering. I brought in my sodden notebooks from the terrace.

Somewhere over in his wing the hollow clatter of a loose shutter; watching the drive through the ridged glass of the front door, I stood in the high hall; the white shelves, niches, sconces, still empty after all these tears, and at first I thought it must have been hidden, I could not find the light-switch, but on a lower shelf, the dull glimmer of the mother-of-pearl.

It is strange that over the years I had not thought more often about the casket, and it is only now when I am certain what it contains that I must confirm my suspicions. I shake the box, and hear the light rattle of photographs, and the wings of the sea pigeons trapped in the chimney we had never used, and I am standing again in that dim airless room among the antique cameras, and the tripods and flaps, a willow-sheltered pond, a balustrade under snow-turbaned mountains, in the wardrobe the row of wire hangers, unzipped suit-bags, on the shelves the card pages of the albums empty but for the plastic corners and dark rectangles like groundplans for buildings never constructed, and I smell the oil and dried blood in the deserts where all is preserved until the end of the ages.

I do not want him to see what I have done when he returns. I will find something thin and hard. There will be no scratches around the lock.

I go through the kitchen which the nurses have re-ordered, and through the racks in the garage, the tool-kits in their shrivelled plastic wrappings. I find a file fine enough.

The lid lifts first time, but I am disappointed. There is no evidence of war crimes, nothing even to hide away from a child, just a couple of old family photographs. My father and my mother when younger, arm in arm under the terrace of the villa, her hair still full and golden as poured honey, the eyes the same candid cornflower as in the later picture in my room; the frame lopsided, his stance off kilter; he has just run round from setting the automatic shutter, and I have never seen him smile so guilessly; the pool was full then, and there were vine trellises over the verandah, and a high wall between the drive and the carretera.

The rain has eased. I go out to the poolhouse to search for cigarettes, and it is only when I turn back towards the house that I realise there is something odd about the photographs, and as I stand on the lower lawn from where the camera must have been positioned I notice the verandah is lower, and at a different angle to the french windows, and there is no view of the drive. That had not been our house.

I take the pictures out into the light, and look again closely, and there over the high wall in the background is an olive terrace, and among the trees I can just make out a small square of colour, a red-and-white fellah headscarf.

In the wind the photographs spin over the wet tiles, as if a tornado had gathered up the house and the gardens and the island and all I had ever known, and set it down again intact at my feet, my world destroyed and recreated as a single drop of rain runs down the window-pane, and for the first time I understood why he had only ever spoken of his brother, and why as a boy I had always been sent to my room when the two beggars called, and why on the steps when he handed them the money they had always addressed him as Pascal.

I lined up three chairs from the corridor, and slept under my coat at the end of the bed. He never regained consciousness.

The road to the Cementerio Nuevo above Bellamar had not been asphalted; the ruts flooded by the rains; the western quadrangle for the Protestants divided from the vacant lower plots by an unpainted breeze-block wall; in the corner between two young cypresses, the enclosure for the other denominations.

A sheer drop to the ring-road, and on the far side the old urbanisation of La Virginia where I had first dined with Sylvie.

At first I assumed there must be another interment being held. I had expected no one, but a small crowd was gathered under the trees; as if his isolation had been an illusion also.

155

They were mostly women. I recognised one of the nurses, a non-playing member from the club, the maid whose dog he had shot that first summer; Foley's mother under a stagey mantilla glistening like a fishing net.

The Greek Orthodox priest had come from the mainland. He arrived last, his censer swinging wildly in the driving wind.

His words lost in the rush of a downpour; the hole covered with a square of fake grass like an indoor putting-run; in the shelter of the wall I shook the hands of the strangers filing back under their umbrellas along the water-logged path to their cars.

I waited until everyone had left, and walked down; one woman had waited behind, by the gate. She was wearing a light raincoat, the collar turned up.

She had grown her hair again, the wind pushing thick strands across her unmade-up face. She kept her hands in her pockets, not lifting the wisps from her eyes.

I do not remember what we said at first. We drove down to find the bar in the urbanisation closed, and later on the front at a hotel cafeteria we drank cortados into the evening, and Anna told me she had come out with a lover to show her the old house, but they had argued and she had left, and afterwards we strolled along the promenade of dirty palms and closed-up kiosks, across the shell-and-anchor paving, stepping between the colours like superstitious children; through the rain-clouds over the straits, our island moon.

1993–1997

I

When an ancient queen was entombed, her most faithful servant was buried alive in the sepulchre. For two decades my father had inhabited her mausoleum, his voice as that of one who spoke from beyond the grave.

For so long I had lived as if he had already died. The Muhammadans say 'He who breeds never dies', but I had deprived him of the comfort of glimpsing his lost love in the eyes of a granddaughter, and had returned his words with silence.

By an infernal calculus, the addict perpetually postpones the day of his deliverance, not because the intensity of his vice is such that he cannot forgo its pleasures, not because he fears the pains of withdrawal; he can only conceive that day as to come, his deliverance eternally deferred.

Many times I had mourned my father before he died, and in his passing I would not find what already had long been lost.

Sylvie had allowed for no rehearsal of mourning. She wrote no signs to augur her parting. She may herself not have anticipated her leaving; she may have known of her leaving so long she had prepared to conceal signs from the very first day we met, our years together no more than an extended prelude to that moment.

It was not so much that she had gone, but that other

presences had intervened, apparitions, memories, crushing the air from my lungs; and finally Anna.

Since we had returned from the island she had taken it upon herself to look after me, telephoning each evening she does not bring round churros and vegetables curries, dragging me out to the openings and launches she covers in her magazine diary.

She had remembered that I had once played tennis; she secured debenture tickets from Bloom for the semi-final between Becker and Stich, the heads of the crowd turning in time, a thousand metronomes; after the first monotonous serve-and-volley set, among the braying tables in the hospitality tent, calling his secretary to hear if there had been developments from Israel.

Bloom's contacts in Tel Aviv had located only two Angelica Bernhardts, one a thirty-year-old officer in the Shin Beth, the other a holocaust survivor, but finding no record of her death had promised to continue the searches.

Slim and dainty as a vanity-flip, she snaps shut her mobile-telephone, and we go to look for her black Renault in the grass lot. She always forgets where she has parked.

Her flat is in that final enclave of low-rent mansion blocks and benefit-hostels being redeveloped by her father's company. The street calls itself a garden; the only vegetation the rotten window-boxes on the pigeon-spattered ledges; her walk-up, the mansard of a rooming-house like the setting for a novel by Muriel Spark, on the ground floor Polish war-veterans, and above batty Irish ladies who are afraid to go out on to the street; she buys in their provisions.

On the stairs and landings, always rolls of lino, wallpaper, pots of paint, the apartments being refurbished after the sitting-tenants have died off or been moved on into nursing-homes.

It is the flat of someone who spends little time at home,

curdled milk and mould-scabbed yoghurt in the fridge, on the sideboard glass vases filled with pond-grey water and still-wrapped sprays of dead roses, the sitting-room given over to a ripped ironing-board and over the chaise-longue and armchairs tin-foil take-away containers used as ashtrays, the radiators hung with shrivelled jeans and T-shirts; the windows unwashed, the only view the dark and narrow street which rarely saw the sun.

The only traces of her former butch phases: in the corner the dumb-bells draped with more drying clothes, on the mantelpiece, the girl with cropped hair and toned forearms hidden like an embarrassing schoolfriend behind the invitations.

On the lime-painted plank that did for a desk, her Amstrad word-processor; above on the pin-board, the originals of the cartoons that accompany her Ozbar magazine diary: a scalped troll in a rubber dress, her hollow skull sprouting a carrot frizz; a gangling giant, sunken-eyed, an Atlas staggering under the mighty orb of his ego; a neon rictus.

Skye; Foley; Michael-Jon.

She stops in the flat only long enough to wash and change, a flapper blithely nosing forward through those elements to which she is indifferent towards some concealed but imminent elation, down between the obstacle-course of paint-pots and dustsheets to search for her car.

But her tales of the Ozbar were mere historical fictions. When there were no parties or openings we returned to my old street; the buzzer broken, no doorman on the landing; the door-hinges still unrepaired from an earlier raid, the rooms above almost always deserted.

The long hall lay in darkness, stripped of the empire couches and chandeliers, drifting away from the city like an ark of the damned, the shredded rugs eddying in the winds through the broken windows; the steet-lights reflecting in the scraps of foil strewn over the bare boards, around the petering fire a huddle of lean men in puffer-jackets sifting the embers with shards of broken furniture; in the windowless dog-leg passage to the bedroom, Palgrave standing his vigil with a tattooed pit bull terrier.

'As if it isn't hard enough already,' as she always said.

Having returned from his stint as private secretary to Quentin Crisp with his head still shaved, he had not ventured to publish his poetry for fear that his grandmother might learn his true opinions on Harrogate, and had been hired as a security-guard on condition he did not open his mouth.

As if below a bullet-grooved parapet, Rustum crouching under the window-sill with his glass pipe and binoculars, peering through a slit in the curtains down the length of the street.

He would insist what he saw was no coincidence. Two of the overlooking flats had the same spider-plants in their windows, the building van parked opposite had smoked-glass windows; a black saloon passed on the hour. But looking down I smelt only the coming winter; those late back from work walking with heads down and shoulders hunched, the street-lights smudged by the mist.

Since Foley had fallen out with Skye, after the inter-national success of the Duplex Sequence and her degree show, she would always be walked by Reaper, and appearing more regularly in the press they could no longer afford to be recognised in such circumstances, and would venture no further than the washroom on the first landing where they would be sorted by one of the lean men from the hall before hastily leaving again.

When we meet old friends we are in effect making new ones, and though the trio continued to make brief appearances at the apartment they would carry themselves with the casual insolence of those who have arrived in a place only to leave, and for whom everything there still appears strange and faintly ridiculous.

Among the tumble-driers and rows of unopened washing-powder, the after-hours art aficionados would congregate in the hope of an informal debate with the controversial painter, but the lack of light and his choice of hats and scarves hid his vulpine face, and before they had realised who they had just been talking to he had already departed.

My rooms were only across the square and the green beyond the railway arches, but when we had scored our wrap and stone we would return to her flat in Kensington.

The Mau with white filigrees on the legs would always remind me of Cancan, and I told her I was allergic to cats, and she would jam the bedroom door with her last diary, and drape a watered-silk scarf over the lamp, and after we had shared the glass pipe and talked of everything except Sylvie we would come down together, burrowing close under the sweat-fug of the duvet as if before a long hibernation; a blanket thrown over the curtains to shut out the morning noises, the hard winter light.

When a woman loses her beauty she may retire from the world, the memory of her prime remaining pristine; if she impersonates her former self like an ageing actress, her beauty will be forgotten, but like the chatelaine of a crumbling mansion Anna inhabited the ruins of her beauty with pride.

Her belly, a paper crumpled in anger, then straightened. I follow and touch-read every line until she is all face to me. She does not watch in the mirror, hide behind hosiery and practised poses; the dropped heft of her breasts, the purled scars of her biking accident.

Her body sculpted by the hands of past lovers, kneaded, pounded, struck, and by their hands held in her hands, and in her strokes and grasps I find the lineaments of these lost legions of which she will never speak.

She says, 'Only the rituals whose meaning has been forgotten are to be observed,' and so I do not understand when she lies with her neck exposed over the edge of the bed as if waiting for a blade to fall, and why she must draw blood and tear licks from the fringe above my bruised lips before she will shudder like a fish drowning in air.

When she is spent, she turns from the coming light, buries herself like a cat licking at my damp lap, not trading secrets like other lovers, whispering only of nights as a girl at the house of her mother on the Norfolk Broads, under the skeletons of the abandoned water-mills the torches of the marshmen, on invisible waters beyond the clogged sluices the black sails of the last wherry, and out in the reedlands the boom of the night-ravens; along the treacherous shore winking light-ships.

Her only picture memory before you were born, but the pram that awaited you already stood down in the hall, pitch and upright like a child's coffin, and smelling of silk umbrellas long out in the rain, and by telling me of what you never saw she will never still your ghost for it is only through my medium that she can suffer your love.

She would like me to believe that you are the skin through which I had always sought her heart; she says I had looked as if at an unfading canvas to be guarded from thieves, but you were only that forgery by which the thieves had concealed your disappearance, and again I cannot write with her words making a trap of our past, and know only that if you discover what has happened I will have lost you for ever.

In the evenings I no longer go out with Anna, to the launches she covers for her column, to the duplex abandoned to the elements. When she calls with curries and churros I do not answer the door.

I fear that if I tell her that I will not bear to see her, she will terminate the continuing enquiries of her father, and so I make my excuses.

Fevers; pressing business affairs on the island; demanding aunts. Of course she suspects there is someone else; on this matter a woman never errs.

All afternoon our telephone conversations like bad sex, hours and hours before she will finish, afterwards an exhaustion that drains the taste from my food, the colour from the flickering screen.

In the phantasmagoria of her column the duplex is still a swirling hub of fire-eaters and playboys and masquers, our fictional selves returning through her flapper dawn to champagne breakfasts and eternal vows, but each night she throws stones at my windows, she scratches my car, she wails on the pavement like a derelict.

During the winter I had already promised to accompany her on a planned trip of Ozbar-veterans to the Yemen; Gervase was to study the weave of the local burnous and abaya; Skye would sketch the traditional fabrics and dyes, Reaper her chaperone; Foley would paint the deserts. Only Rustum would not leave his redoubt, Palgrave remaining to care for him.

Each night I worked on my excuses, but could confect nothing she had not heard before, until on the morning of our departure I received a call from the office of her father; after the death of her husband, Walter, Angelica Bernhardt had married a school principal from Nazareth, and was now living in a large walled house in the hills west of Jerusalem.

II

It is raining in Jerusalem.

I sit at the nearest table to the door, in the lobby the two clerks behind the desk watching the raindrops down the tinted-glass swing-doors; beyond in the corridor the Arab cleaning-women dragging their long mops as if guiding invisible barges.

Beside the kosher buffet, the queue of businessmen passes slowly, like a gameshow where the contestants must remember every item before they can take them home; on one plate, a high pile of cold beef, chicken-legs, gherkins, sardines; over the rim, crème-caramel, sorbet, chocolate gâteau. When I reach the table I must make do with rice and flan.

The King David Hotel had been taken over by a diplomatic convention, and so the associates of Bloom had booked me into the Moriah Palace on the Mamilla Road. From my balcony on the fifth floor I had a view over the grid of pre-war grey-stone villas with their walled orchards and gardens built by the Christian families who had prospered under the British Mandate; across the road, an office building once owned by our family, the rose-red columns quarried from the Petra deserts glowing like embers in the setting sun; to the rear the monumental façade of the YMCA.

Everywhere I had the sense I was being followed, so little of the city of my father's stories had survived that wherever I walked the amber of his memories seemed no more than a garbled and fanciful rendering of a species long extinct; St Stephen's Gate, a busy thoroughfare; the gardens of the German Colony lying unkempt with the reproachful air of a place nobody heeded any more.

All that second afternoon I waited, and when the driver came he said the old lady was still not ready to receive me, and so in the evening when the rain had eased I walked up the quiet boulevards of Mamilla to where the house of my grandparents had once stood, across the roundabout the windmill planted with geraniums as my father had described, a gauze of cloud over the moon, the view over the old walls and the dome obscured by another new hotel whose name I have forgotten.

Between the rubbish-strewn lots and cattle-pens, I climbed on into the scrubland, wandering over damp grass and wild flowers, through the drizzle-dark gulleys, moonlight on water, the lit grids of the sleeping city.

On the third day the rain had continued all morning; I had waited in my room for the driver; he had come in a larger saloon. We took the main road out through the hills to the west of the city. He had not pulled aside the Perspex screen, and I could not hear what he was saying, and nodded and smiled whenever his voice turned to a crescendo.

Up an unasphalted lane, between staggered new housing-developments built over levelled olive terraces. On the heights, the windows narrowed to arrow-slits, the flat roofs castellated, plastic star-of-David pennants and blue-dyed sheets fluttering on the water-towers.

At the end of the lane, high walls topped with broken glass and razor-wire; the reinforced gates double-chained; a sense of fortification, and imprisonment.

The driver cannot find a buzzer; he knocks on the gate

167

without response. He returns to the car, and rings from the portable under the console.

From behind a buttress of cement sacks, an old man with a rank beard and a spade under his arm had appeared briefly, peered down the track as if at his first view of a foreign land, and closed the door again.

I had crossed the lane with my few rehearsed words of greeting in Hebrew, and the door had opened, and there was a menacing wave of the spade; a spatter of phlegm landing on my trouser-leg.

For half an hour the driver stood in the rain, his words lost in the wind, a builder coming out from the shells of the garages, cupping his hands as he calls towards the car, all the time the water-logged cement-spills creeping like lava across the lane.

It was already dusk as we returned between the brightly lit pavement cafés of the new city. The old Arab husband had mistaken me for a settler, the builder had told the driver, the Jewish Sitt was as old as the century, and could do nothing for herself, though it was said among the barakiyat down by the well under the last terrace that the Ustaz still loved her for what she had been, and would allow no nurses or maids into the house, bed-washing her, carrying her with him into each room, playing music late into the night though she could no longer speak or hear; the domestic provisions lowered in baskets over the high wall.

Of the previous occupants of the house the builders had known nothing, though the old fellahin still told tales of a golden-haired houri wandering the wild gardens.

On my return from Jerusalem there were no messages from Anna. A week later Skye called asking how she could contact her. From her feigned lack of interest it was evident she thought I knew more than I would tell her.

Anna had flown back early from the Yemen trip due to

168

her morning-sickness; she had not been at her flat. No one could find her.

An hour later Reaper had telephoned from Skye's flat in Notting Hill, where he had been staying since renting Church Street to Rose, with a cock-eyed story about Anna being paid a six-figure sum to bear a child for Don Luis. I had already dismissed the phantom pregnancy as no more than an excuse to pull out of the trip, a canard to cover a new affair.

A month afterwards Foley had dropped round to ask if I would write a catalogue essay for his forthcoming Temple Beggar Sequence, and as always I had refused; I had never understood his work. It was only out of politeness so as not to end the visit too peremptorily that he had mentioned in passing how he had glimpsed Anna a few weeks before in a Soho club; he put it down to her having come off drugs that she had filled out so much.

The moment he had left I went round to the flat in South Kensington, and when no one answered the buzzer waited outside in the car for three hours; upstairs, the curtains open, no lights on.

After four days of enquiries by his security men, Shaman rang back to assure me she was not on the island. That evening I drove up to Norfolk, diverting to eat at a fish restaurant in Manningtree which I had chanced upon long ago with Sylvie in those months she would blindly throw darts at the map to divine our weekend destination, but when finally late at night I came to the village where the house of their mother had once stood I found only a double silo above a sluicing caisson, the surrounding wetlands drained, on every side seas of green wheat reaching out to a horizon level and flat as the graph-line of an unbeating heart.

As depravity for some insecure persons is little more in origin than a mask from which the weak derive the security of an identity, albeit a dubious one, allowing the wearer to recognise himself in others, and find acceptance among their number, so for such false sybarites the sudden transition to abstinence and conventionality is not only always achieved to the astonishment of all, but with a spritely facility which would be an agony for the truly depraved.

Like signature phrases or gestures, clothes worn too often soon become invisible, and so when they are dropped it seems the man we knew also has disappeared.

After the failure of his stateside franchises Gervase had rented out his flat, and was living in reduced circumstances, looking to borrow money, and a place to stay, but I did not return his calls.

Whenever I tried to write I found myself looking at whatever part of the room I had hidden your unanswerable letters; I packed them in a jiffy-bag, posted them to the offices of the abogado on the island.

That summer I stayed in my rooms, disconnecting the telephone. Blocking the light through the windows, the packing-cases from the island, unopened; over the floors the spill of polythene balls like the white mints left to sweeten the cheque; spawns of bubble-wrap.

Sometimes now when the afternoon is not too clammy I cross the green beyond the pool-hall and take the long way round to the rear of Oxford Gardens. Through the railway arches behind Esmond Square, along the perimeter of the estate, and down as far as the corner of Willow Mews where there is the usual spill-over of late-lunchers and afternoon drinkers on the pavement outside the Toad-in-the-Hole; from here there is a clear view up to the back windows of the upper storey of the duplex.

Although the panes have not been washed for years, in the mid-afternoon when the sun has passed over the house it is still possible to have a plain view of any movement near the windows. But the thick sage curtains are always partially drawn, only a narrow gap between the frayed linings, and by aligning myself in the same position between the stoop and the fallow half-barrel I have been able to verify that this gap remains constant, and subsequent visits have confirmed that the curtains on that side of the house are never touched.

The rain has passed, the sky suddenly so bright it seems impossible to believe night will ever fall again.

Later I will draw out the walk back from the pub. There is an almost Mediterranean languor in the late summer streets, the few who are out moving like stunned flies, in the hallways of hostels old men looking out into the tired light, children listlessly circling on mountain-bikes, through the empty estate bare-backed girls drifting towards the park.

Sometimes I walk beyond the garages beneath the railway arches where work has stopped for the day and come out above the old canal; down along the banks, debris thrown free from the centrifuge of the city, trolleys, bent bicycle-wheels, half-prams, scattered like the wreckage of a blast.

A single ramshackle barge beneath the converted ware-houses, their brightly painted brickwork unseasonally festive above the sullen water; far below, the cars like ants over newsprint; along the sunless avenues, the winding way to the twin-towers above my rooms.

I had become a stranger by staying where I was. In the stillness of the afternoons, memories of the old neighbour-hood, derelict squares, hardboard-fronted shebeens, pubs with blackened windows; after a rough night on the floor of the Tennants' rambling house on Camden Hill Square, wandering down the hill with Palgrave into this wild west to score some blow to take back to school, carrying shopping bags so we would look like locals; the new house of his sister in Chesterton Road had seemed like the end of the world, the door never locked, on the ground floor a confusion of half-scraped walls and planks and paint-spattered sofas where we would shelter to have our first smoke, relieved we had not been clipped; from somewhere higher up where we never ventured, a distant and fretful moaning like a slow birth.

But now I go out and no longer recognise where I am; stage-sets for short-run productions, the bistros and boutiques with their ethnic façades and abstract names constantly shifting; on the pavements sons in the suits of their fathers, mothers in the dresses of their daughters, those younger than myself in the clothes I had always been too young to wear.

On the streets I am walking down into my own past, they have built the city from their mirrors. In every newsagent, corner shop, high-hoarding, kiosk, underground escalator: their faces. They are the deities over the crossroads, carriageway shrines; their blind eyes watching the overpasses and the short-cuts, and the path along the canal.

Rose in Skye's dresses.

Skye in Rose's arms.

Anna as the naked Christ, arms spread over the last supper.

When I meet someone I knew from the old days, they hug me, not to welcome me back, but as if I was setting out on a long journey.

And why in this age of mass reproduction and seriality must we still value what we own as unique when it can be replaced in perfect duplicate within hours, for are we not like the fellahin who believe the old stones bear the spirits of those who died amongst their ruin, absorbing invisibly all we have done these dumb witnesses to our lives we keep like household gods, and estimate their silence.

I thought I had found all his letters, but like bones on an old battlefield they still turn up in the furrows of my shortened days.

On the back-deck I empty the black earth from the largest

172

urn. Single sheets at first, the fire slow to catch. After the letters, my old reading-lists, like the debts of Third-World countries, multiplying until they must be written off.

Her stickered-over sketch-books, the hesitant bowls of fruit, wilting lilies, a fallen roemer glass; some pages torn out; acts of destruction, or preservation?

My own notebooks, sand-stuck pages, schoolboy renderings from her books of poetry; from Heine, Celan; from Trakl.

Und leise tönen im Rohr die dunkeln flöten des Herbstes.

And in the reeds mutter the dark flutes of autumn.

Through the high column of smoke, the lights across the city dull as fallen coins.

The summer is always ending. Against the darkening panes, the buzz and fizzle of dying flies; the hiss of the frying from the back-yard of the Aphrodite.

And later there will be the cooing of pigeons, the calling of children from the green, tonight I will listen for them, and you will remember perhaps the seasons of the city passing one into the other as two deserts embracing; this halcyon light through the thinning trees.

The sun white through her hair in those first colour photographs.

Some summers have ended before they began, others drifting on into the autumn, late island summers.

The Catherine wheel of the seasons spinning ever faster; a perpetual August, everyone still away, the city to yourself again.

At lunchtime I no longer cross to the Kleftiko; no longer take down the rubbish-bags.

They leave what I have ordered in the hall. They come and go silent and unseen, as if I were that eighteenth-century lord who would sack his servants on sight, his lawns mown by night.

Newspapers, mezze; cigarettes. One by one the rooms

173

filled by the black polythene sacks, reefs of yellowing paper; a flat of bunkers and trenches.

When I look out to a dark window, no empty room, but someone spying unseen. All day I sleep, and at night I read only to find the one line that will forgive everything.

III

A blinding shimmer over the long caterpillar-pavilion built on the lawn outside the museum. But I have come to the wrong place. The commissionaire in his gloves and epaulettes tells me Skye's show has been relocated to a former slaughterhouse in Clerkenwell.

In the taxi I study the invitation again. On the back, a list of celebrity models: Rose Lovell, Imam, Anna Bloom; the photograph of a chained manikin in drooping hipsters; I must sit close to make out the stretch-marks, the Caesarean-line.

But when I arrive the show is over, the road blocked by the ladders of the cameramen, white ropes strung between gilded posts; over the walls, the strobe of muzzle-flashes.

Past the suited bouncers, through the lobby crush, up narrow stairs to a gangway, but the hall below is empty; on either side the chairs in disarray, the catwalk crossed with fallen streamers and paper blooms.

Beneath the last guests are leaving, two wheelchairs descending the ramp like rides at a funfair waiting to pick up speed.

Through the wrought-iron lattice I watch as they pass under me into the entrance-hall. In the first, Rustum, shrivelled and drug-smiling like a palsy child; over horn-handles, Palgrave's bobbing skinhead.

And last, an old man, his pitted face like a rotten walnut, the pale woman pushing too slight to manage the incline of the ramp.

But you were only using one hand, the other fumbling for your soft-pack. If you had looked up you would not have seen me, reaching also for my cigarettes, and turning my face to the wall.

It was growing dark by the time I had found a taxi, the traffic slow towards Piccadilly. Above on the blocks between Regent Street and Shaftesbury Avenue the still fire of trade-names and digital countdowns; the circus empty of its central statue.

I asked the driver where the Cupid had gone. He pointed back towards the wide mainland of pavement beyond the Criterion Restaurant, tourists with cameras and boys with beer-cans milling around the black margin, and against the sepia sky the winged god with his outstretched bow diving like a great bird of prey over the square.

You could open the curtains now. Below the terrace, a sagging water-logged net, drizzle-blurred service-lines on the clay court over the concrete-filled pool; the last view through to the breakwater lost to the high rear-walls of the techno club and the fitness centre.

On these wet days, the instructors do not come up for a set, and under the rain-swept french windows at the desk you never used I sit all day, and write this journal; not the book you would have wanted written, only the record of the failure to write that book.

You told me in this life all our desires are fulfilled on condition they do not bring the happiness we expected of them.

And still sometimes in those late summers when I returned from the island Sylvie would drive in from the house Don Luis had bought by the river at Richmond and we would meet in the afternoons at a cinema in Kensington or Notting Hill Gate, and always she brought her baby boy swaddled in a hooded anorak despite the heat, and afterwards we would sit out what time we had left in a coffee bar and stroll in the park.

And from the railings I watch as they walk down between the line of beeches to the road, the face of the little boy staring back under the fur fringes of the hood as she turns his head towards a kite riding in the gusts above the trees.

A NOTE ON THE AUTHOR

Born in Beirut, Tony Hanania was brought up in the Lebanon and educated in England. He now lives in West London. He is the author of *Homesick*, shortlisted for the John Llewellyn Rhys Prize, and *Unreal City*, and was a recipient of the London Arts Board New Writer's Award.

A NOTE ON THE TYPE

The text of this book is set in Linotype Janson. The original types were cut in about 1690 by Nicholas Kis, a Hungarian working in Amsterdam. The face was misnamed after Anton Janson, a Dutchman who worked at the Ehrhardt Foundry in Leipzig, where the original Kis types were kept in the early eighteenth century.

Monotype Ehrhardt is based on Janson. The original matrices survived in Germany and were acquired in 1919 by the Stempel Foundry. Herman Zapf used these originals to redesign some of the weights and sizes for Stempel. This Linotype version was designed to follow the original types under the direction of C. H. Griffith.